THE GUIDE TO LARRY NIVEN'S RINGWORLD

THE GUIDE TO LARRY NIVEN'S RINGWORLD

KEVIN STEIN

ILLUSTRATED BY
TODD HAMILTON
JAMES CLOUSE

DESIGN AND LAYOUT
KEVIN STEIN

PRODUCTION JULIAN JACKSON

THE GUIDE TO LARRY NIVEN'S RINGWORLD

This is a work of fiction. All the characters and events portrayed in this book are fictional, and any resemblance to real people or incidents is purely coincidental.

Copyright © 1994 by Bill Fawcett & Associates under license from New Frontier Entertainment

All rights reserved, including the right to reproduce this book or portions thereof in any form.

A Baen Books Original

Baen Publishing Enterprises
P.O. Box 1403
Riverdale, NY 10471

ISBN: 0-671-72204-2

Cover art by David Mattingly

First printing, February 1994

Distributed by Paramount
1230 Avenue of the Americas
New York, NY 10020

Library of Congress Cataloging-in-Publication Data

Stein, Kevin
THE GUIDE TO LARRY NIVEN'S RINGWORLD
p. cm.
ISBN 0-671-72192-5 : $20.00
1. Niven, Larry. Ringworld—Dictionaries. 2. Science fiction, American—Dictionaries. I. Niven, Larry. Ringworld. II. Title.

PS3564.I9Z87 1994   93-35023
813'.54—dc20   CIP

Though the *Ringworld* is a very personal vision, it has always had an aspect of collaboration. I finished the calculations for its spin while visiting some friends, borrowing their books to find the formulas. Lectured a Bay area science fiction club on the structure, that night. A stranger in Washington, DC, proof-read the first edition ("The Niven/MacArthur Papers, volume 1") and found an amazing number of mistakes for us. The back covers of the fanzine *APA-L* for many months featured Ringworld puns, or Ringworlds with printing across the underside. "One Ring to Rule Them All." "Occupancy by more than 3×10^{15} persons is dangerous and unlawful."

At the 1971 World Science Fiction Convention, MIT students chanted in the Hilton halls: "The Ringworld is unstable!"

The best hard-SF artists have tried their skills on the Ringworld.

In 1970 the Ringworld was the strangest engineering feat since Dante's *Divine Comedy*. I feared it would be too off-the-wall. On the contrary, it seems just strange enough to stretch most minds, and just simple enough that everyone thinks he can improve it.

And the improvements flow in.

—The flup/spillpipe/spill mountain system came from a high school class in Florida (and made Ringworld mining rights possible).
—The shadow square system provides too much twilight. For proper day and night, use five long rectangles orbiting *retrograde*.
—Why settle for shadow squares? Build a balloon out of solar power collector material, the size of the orbit of Mercury. No spin needed. Furnish with radiator fins, a power beam system, windows along the waist. The sun goes at the center.

Solar gravity—which is powerful enough to collapse a *real* Dyson sphere—is balanced by sunlight falling on the inside. You use all of the output of the sun for industrial power—as with a Dyson sphere. The windows allow sunlight for the Ringworld, and also allow attitude control.

—Two weeks ago, at the second DCX rocket test flight, one of the rocket scientists spoke to me thus. He and some companions believe that the proper diameter for the Ringworld is a million miles (width is optional, as usual). At that size, a 24-hour rotation provides one gravity. You don't even need "scrith"; predictable materials, such as cable made from Fullerite carbon tubes, would be strong enough.

As always, I most appreciate the reader who gets the most out of the story. You never have to stop with just reading the book. A story is an intellectual playground too; and I like to leave the gates open when I leave.

What can you do with the Ringworld, that the author didn't think of? Don't violate my copyrights, please; don't break the equipment. But it is a playground. So play.

Larry Niven

TABLE OF CONTENTS

9	INTRODUCTION TO RINGWORLDS
10	HISTORY OF KNOWN SPACE
27	MAJOR RACES OF KNOWN SPACE
76	ALIENS OF KNOWN SPACE
101	THE RINGWORLD
126	RACES OF RINGWORLD
161	PSIONICS
165	EQUIPMENT
182	GLOSSARY

INTRODUCTION TO RINGWORLDS

Ringworld is an artificial habitat that surrounds its sun. A good deal of sunlight is converted into energy for use on the surface of the ring. Other than Niven, there have been three other significant futurists who decided that any advanced industrial society must eventually build its own world surrounding its sun to gather the greatest amount of raw energy, the most important resource (other than matter and living space) to any expanding civilization.

In 1895, Constantin Tsiolkovski envisioned in his *Dreams of Earth and Sky* a cloud of space cities built from asteroids given atmospheres and water. These bubble-domed habitats orbited around the sun, harvesting light for the benefit of the city's inhabitants.

N.S. Kardeshev extended Tsiolkovski's ideas by creating subdivisions of technological societies: Type I, II, and III. Type I civilizations could reconfigure the surface of worlds, "terraforming" them for eventual population. Type II societies had the ability to transform solar systems. Type III civilizations could harness the matter and energy output of entire galaxies.

Freeman Dyson said that, "One should expect within a few thousand years of entering the stage of industrial development, any intelligent species should be found occupying an artificial biosphere which completely surrounds its parent star." The idea of a Dyson Sphere has become a hallmark of science fiction, a hollow, spherical shell built around a star to make use of every photon of light. The mass of a planet the size of Jupiter could be used to create a Dyson sphere several meters thick with the diameter of one Earth orbit.

The interior of a Dyson Sphere has billions of times the surface area of Earth. However, gravity generators must be emplaced all over the shell to ensure that nothing falls into the sun, including the atmosphere; there is no night, only the constant day of the sun overhead. The rest of the universe is hidden.

Ringworld takes care of the major problems encountered with building a Dyson Sphere (other than the actual construction itself, of course). A ring built around the sun with the same resources would be tens of meters thick, a million kilometers wide, and a billion kilometers long. The surface area would still be immense, and the ring can be spun to create artificial gravity through centrifugal force. Building a ringworld also takes care of one more important problem close to every romantic's heart.

You can see the stars.

HISTORY OF KNOWN SPACE

- **11**   History of Known Space
- **16**   Timeline of Known Space
- **19**   Maps of Known Space
- **21**   Worlds of Known Space

HISTORY OF KNOWN SPACE

One of the greatest discoveries of the late 20th century was the tenth planet, named Persephone. This inspired the newly unified governments of Earth to begin further exploration of the cosmos. They quickly discovered other planets around nearby stars. The stage was set for outreach.

Space exploration was more than just rewarding, it was also an adventure. Theories on physiology and human behavior were overturned by some of the first long-range shuttle flights. Near-space industries, such as low gravity metallurgy, became more than curiosities. The asteroid belt was mined and inhabited by the resourceful and strong-willed.

THE NEW WORLD ORDER

The most prominent challenge to the governments of Earth was the fight against hunger, oppression, and illiteracy. This led to the rededication of the United Nations, which was not a figurehead board of "important" leaders from nations around the world, but a true league that kept sovereignty over the unified countries.

One of the UN's hardest fights was with the Belters, who had declared independence from the Earth. The Belters and Earth waged economic war with each other until the UN recognized the Belt as a separate world government.

This is not to say that the United Nations created a utopia. Many of the people once in power attempted to maintain their holdings through corruption and blackmail. There were incidents of nuclear terrorism. In the end, the strife that rose from the creation of the United Nations served to strengthen its cause and purpose.

THE ARM

The Amalgamation of Regional Militia became the enforcement branch of the UN. As man's level of technology rose under the banner of the new age, the number of possible abuses of the technology rose exponentially. The ARM was there to make sure that nothing got out of control. ARM agents were often sent on missions outside the Earth system.

The ARM performs two major functions. The first is the monitoring of technology. The second is the enforcement of the fertility laws, which kept the Earth from facing overpopulation, famine, and economic disaster. The laws assured that the population stabilized at about eighteen billion people by the 22nd century.

Originally, the ARM also ensured that the organ donation laws were not abused. It was very easy for someone to make a great deal of money by "procuring" organs for organ banks. Unfortunately, these types of donations were not usually voluntary. The ARM no longer needed to enforce these laws when organs were generated in labs.

EARTH'S GOLDEN AGE

The golden age lasted three centuries. Dolphins were admitted to the United Nations. Technology continued to advance for the benefit of society. Psionic skills were catalogued, and some became useful skills. The first transfer booths were created. Current addiction also originated in this era.

The stars beckoned. The UN sent the first robotic fusion ramships to probe the planets of nearby stars. All were programmed to send back information via message laser. Some of the rambots were damaged during the journey and gave poor information, and some vanished. However, the ships sent to Alpha Centauri, Tau Ceti, Epsilon Indi, Sirius, and Procyon found places for humans to live.

SLOWBOATS TO CENTAURI

Slowboats were huge, one hundred meter diameter black cylinders resembling monstrous tuna-cans with beveled edges. The colonists rode in cryogenic suspension, and a crew of four operated the ship during flight.

The slowboat journeys were always one way; if the passengers found problems at their destinations, they had to deal with it themselves, not much of a surprise considering the distance. By the late 22nd century there were at least six colonized worlds with more on the way.

Some of the rambots had sent unreliable information. The colonists on Jinx had to labor under 1.78 gees. We Made It's one thousand kilometer per hour winds meant a spare existence underground. Genetic drift and planetary dangers changed the colonists radically over the centuries.

THE SEA STATUE AND OTHER DISCOVERIES

In 2106, the dolphins found something they called the Sea Statue. It was the first evidence of alien intelligence. The statue was actually a stasis field generator holding one of the long extinct Thrint, also called the Slavers. The Slaver was returned to stasis (with a great deal of difficulty), but it had telepathically given a few scientists a shocking view of the galaxy's past. It also provided a look at undreamed of technology; the Slaver disintegrator was engineered from the telepathic memory implant.

On Jinx that same year, the Bandersnatchi were also found to be intelligent. They had additional memories of the Slaver empire, which convinced the ARM that all significant Slaver findings must be reported or turned over to government authorities. Thrint weapons were too powerful to be allowed in the hands of common society.

Belter Jack Brennan was captured by Phssthpok the Pak in 2125. He was exposed to tree-of-life root and transformed into a protector. He killed Phssthpok and took the alien ramship, issuing a warning to the UN of the Pak's xenophobia.

Phssthpok's mummified body and the Sea Statue are on display, next to each other, at the Smithsonian.

THE MAN-KZIN WARS

Earth had known relative peace for two hundred and fifty years. A great deal of the problems that arose with the advent of new technologies and medical advances had been solved. Colonies no longer had to wait years for new supplies and news from Earth. Everyone wanted to meet an alien species, guessing contact would be friendly and mutually beneficial.

It was not until several years after the initial subjugation of Wunderland that word reached Earth of a Kzinti surprise attack. It was also discovered that the Kzinti often ate the flesh of their victims.

The Kzinti invaded Earth's system and the Belters kept them at bay using laser propulsion drives as weapons. The Kzinti would have eventually won the battle had the Puppeteers not interfered, guiding the Outsiders to the colony of We Made It, where the governor bought the secret of the Quantum I hyperdrive shunt. The hyperdrive armadas drove the Kzinti from Earth.

The Earth armed itself, building greater laser cannons and sending picket ships out into other systems as a first line of defense. In the meantime, interstellar trade flourished since the hyperdrive made it possible to reach another system in days instead of years.

The Outsiders leased a base on Nereid and the Puppeteers made themselves known.

The Kzinti tried to invade the Earth in 2449-2475, 2491-2531, and 2560-2584. There was a final incident in 2651, at which time the Kzinti agreed to what they call the Fourth Truce With Man.

THE PUPPETEERS

Puppeteer technology revolutionized Known Space. Earth had learned to build gravity polarizers from the Kzinti, but they become obsolete when the Puppeteers sold the secret of reactionless thrusters. Pelton Industries was acquired by the General Products corporation and introduced vastly improved transfer booths.

The Puppeteers also influenced the business and personal ethics of many corporations and colonies. They interfered with the Fertility Laws by surreptitiously creating the Birthright Lotteries.

The expedition sponsored by the Puppeteers to the galactic core revealed that the core had exploded, and the resulting shockwave of radiation would kill everything in its path. The Puppeteers immediately pulled out of their business ventures and retreated from the galaxy, creating a stock market crash that nearly spelled the doom for every colony in Known Space.

KNOWN SPACE

Known Space contains the forty light year diameter bubble of Human Space, and all the star systems of the known alien races. There are about ten thousand stars in Known Space, most of which have never been explored. There are thirty billion humans and a smaller number of aliens inhabiting Known Space.

Four new planets have been discovered in Earth's solar system, Persephone, Caina, Antenora, and Ptolomea; they are all gas giants. Venus is undergoing terraforming, but the Moon remains untouched. Mars' 1.1 million inhabitants are confined to their colony sites.

EARTH IN THE 29TH CENTURY

"Flatlander" was once a Belter slur against people who did not or could not travel in space, but is now used to mean "native-born." Most flatlanders are tolerant of other species and "Offworlders," but there is sometimes a hint of xenophobia or disdain when flatlanders encounter other sentient life forms, even if they are from the human colonies.

Earth can seem overcrowded and bland. Some urban centers have blended together, such as San Francisco and San Diego, top and bottom of a huge urban megalopolis. Transfer booths criss-cross the world in a network of instantaneous travel, and slidewalks allow more convenient travel over shorter distances. Interworld has become the standard of language.

Earth itself is actually a wonderland of culture and color. The greatest comforts and luxuries are readily available, as are entertainments and conveniences. The living arcologies are remarkable works of architecture that give the illusion of space and isolation.

Flatlander food is still the best in Known Space.

Most flatlanders never leave the Earth, despite the adventures of space. The most optimistic flatlanders say that the poorest citizen of Earth lives better than most well-off colonists. But some flatlanders cannot resist the lure of travel and the mysteries of the cosmos.

DISCOVERY OF THE RING

Despite the Ringworld's "top secret" status, news of the artifact has reached the fringes of the general public of all known races. The ARM, the Kzinti, and the Puppeteers hold the Ringworld to be a tremendous concern and point of anxiety.

TIMELINE OF KNOWN SPACE

500,000–1,000,000 B.C.	Construction of the Ringworld
1500 B.C.	City Builders became the undisputed masters of a large sector of Ringworld.
1733 A.D.	Superconductor plague is introduced to Ringworld by Experimentalist Puppeteers in a shrewd attempt to offset threatening technology before setting up business relations.
	Conservative Puppeteers seize control of government and decide not to confront Ringworld. They file it away for possible future study.
2040–2099	The United Nations is reorganized into a true World Government of Earth.
	Creation of the high-tech UN police force, The ARM.
	Colonization of the Belt.
	UN-Belt Cooperation Accord.
	Belt sets up independent government.
	Interstellar ram robots launched.
	First colony slowboats launched.
2090–2100	Human colony worlds established on Jinx, We Made It, and Wunderland.
2106	First alien discovered on Earth—a member of the Thrint (Slaver) race, accidentally released from a stasis field.
	Bandersnatchi are discovered on Jinx.
2125	Phssthpok the Pak arrives in the Sol system after traveling 30,000 light years to save humanity.
2189	Human colony established on Home.
2150–2360	The Golden Age on Earth.
2200	Jinx proclaims independence from UN controls.
2351	The Home catastrophe.

2360	First contact with Kzinti.
	Experimentalists regain control of Puppeteer government.
2367	Kzinti attack Alpha Centauri, subjugating Wunderland.
	Institute of Knowledge on Jinx invents Boosterspice.
2410	Humans on We Made It buy hyperdrive engine from Outsider merchants insuring a string of victories by humans over Kzinti.
2420	End of first Man-Kzin War.
	Down is liberated.
	Puppeteers reveal themselves to humanity.
2449–2475	Second Man-Kzin War.
2491–2531	Third Man-Kzin War.
	The Kzin military command planet Canyon is annexed.
2560–2584	Fourth Man-Kzin War.
2589	Home is recolonized.
2590	Puppeteers expand their business empire into Human and Kzin space controlling an ample portion of Known Space commerce.
2640	Puppeteer development of Quantum II hyperdrive.
	Puppeteer-sponsored test flight of the Long Shot, the first ship to utilize the Quantum II hyperdrive, piloted by Beowolf Schaffer. Schaffer takes the craft to the galactic core and discovers the Galactic core explosion is expanding and a cloud of deadly radiation will engulf Known Space in 20,000 years.
	The Puppeteer Exodus.
	Stock Market Crash in human space.

2650	Louis Gridley Wu is born.
	Puppeteer influence amends Fertility Laws by introducing Birthright Lotteries in an attempt to "breed" lucky humans.
2830	Contact with Trinocs.
2850	First expedition to Ringworld; sponsored by the Experimentalist Hindmost.
2851	Conservative Puppeteer party denounces the Ringworld expedition as a total disaster and tosses out the Experimentalist Hindmost. The Conservatives take control of the Puppeteer Fleet-of-Worlds.
2870	Second expedition to Ringworld; a secret mission led by the deposed Experimentalist Hindmost to discover secrets that would reinstate its former status.
2895	The third expedition to Ringworld led by Son-of-Chmee and an ex-ARM agent named Quinn. The Kzin Patriarch has threatened to destroy the Puppeteer Fleet-of-Worlds in retaliation for the Puppeteer's breeding experiments and genocide of the Kzinti race. Quinn and Son-of-Chmee are manipulated by the Puppeteers to destroy the approaching Kzin warship with technology found on the Ringworld.

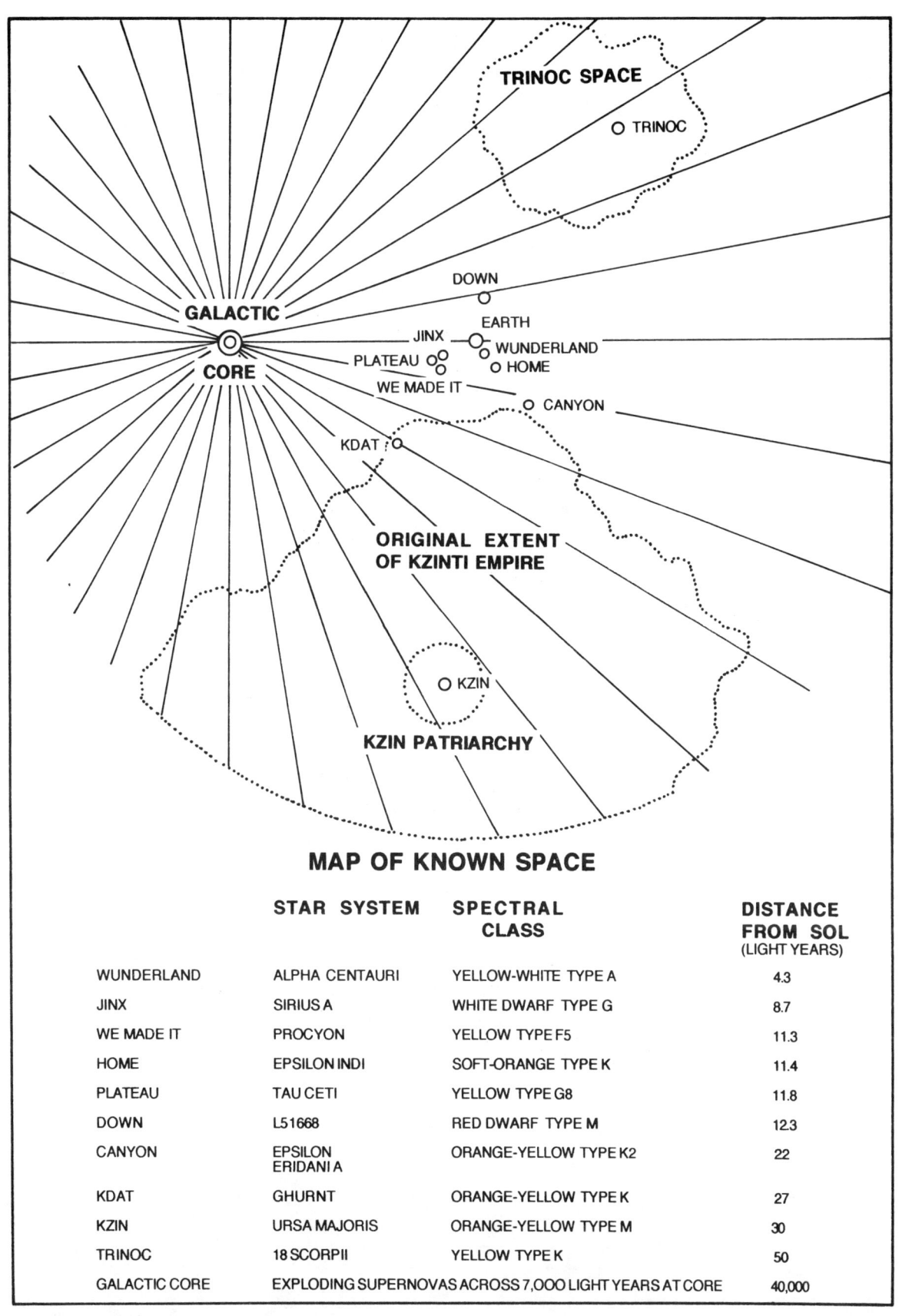

MAP OF KNOWN SPACE

	STAR SYSTEM	SPECTRAL CLASS	DISTANCE FROM SOL (LIGHT YEARS)
WUNDERLAND	ALPHA CENTAURI	YELLOW-WHITE TYPE A	4.3
JINX	SIRIUS A	WHITE DWARF TYPE G	8.7
WE MADE IT	PROCYON	YELLOW TYPE F5	11.3
HOME	EPSILON INDI	SOFT-ORANGE TYPE K	11.4
PLATEAU	TAU CETI	YELLOW TYPE G8	11.8
DOWN	L51668	RED DWARF TYPE M	12.3
CANYON	EPSILON ERIDANI A	ORANGE-YELLOW TYPE K2	22
KDAT	GHURNT	ORANGE-YELLOW TYPE K	27
KZIN	URSA MAJORIS	ORANGE-YELLOW TYPE M	30
TRINOC	18 SCORPII	YELLOW TYPE K	50
GALACTIC CORE	EXPLODING SUPERNOVAS ACROSS 7,000 LIGHT YEARS AT CORE		40,000

History of Known Space — *The Guide to Larry Niven's Ringworld*

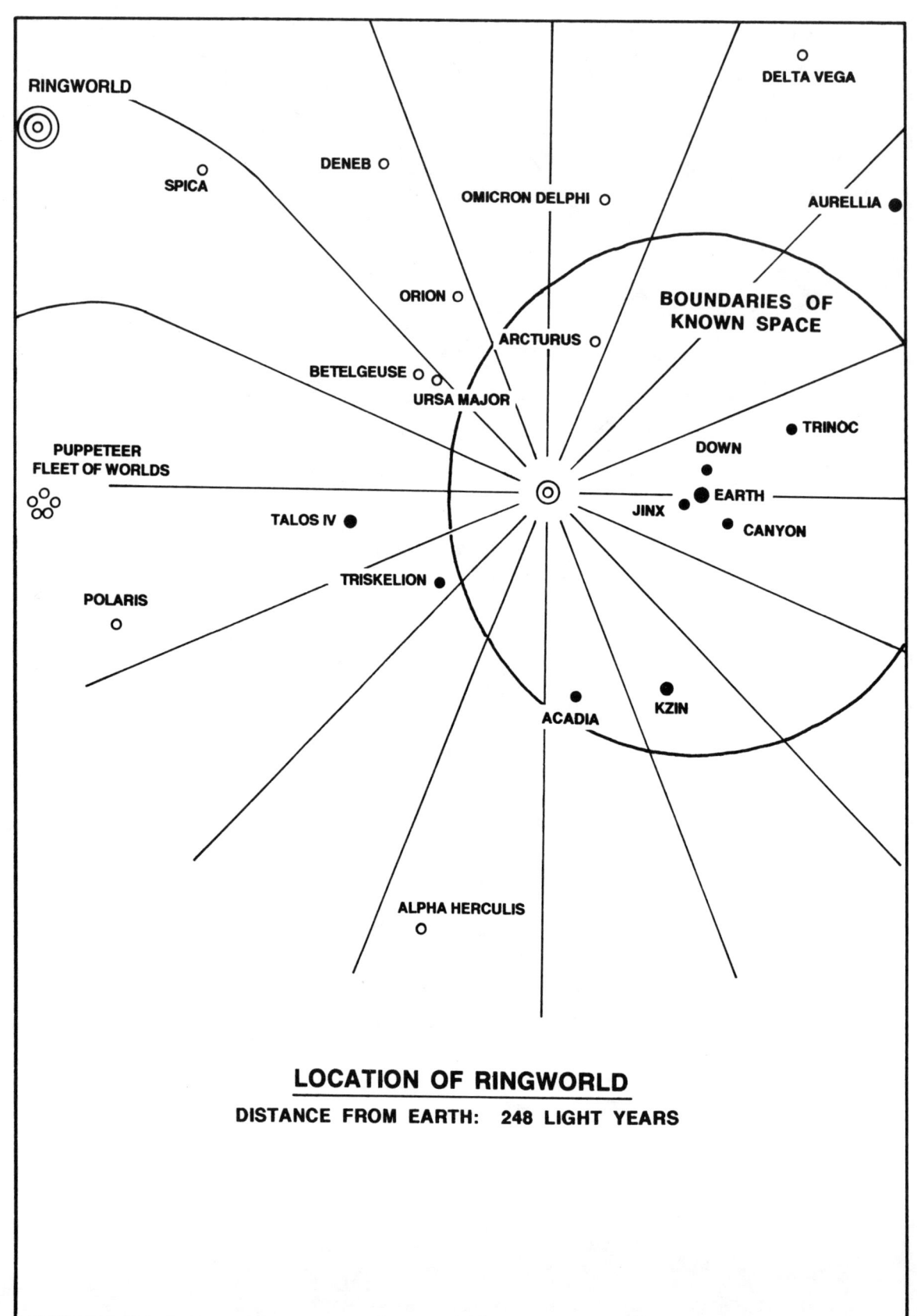

WORLDS OF KNOWN SPACE

CANYON

Canyon marks the southernmost contour of Kzin Space, and has been of invaluable strategic importance in enforcing the UN restrictions on Kzinti expansionism. Formerly a Kzinti world with a substantial military-industrial complex, it was annexed at the close of the Third Man-Kzin War (2531) by the use of an awesome energy weapon called the "Wunderland Treatymaker." This weapon virtually annihilated the Kzinti top military command when the military installation, protected by stasis fields, was swallowed by molten lava in the center of a twelve mile deep gash. The Kzinti generals continue to wait in stasis with their plans for galactic dominance…

System:	e Eridani A
Distance From Sol:	22 light years
Size:	7,715 Kilometers at the Equator. Small, not much bigger than Mars
Surface Gravity:	0.45 gee
Day:	27.1 UNS Hours
Year:	262 UNS Days
Moons:	None
Distance From Primary:	70.7 Million Miles
Chief Industries:	Mining of rich radioactives and high-grade heavy-metal ores.
Atmosphere:	Air pressure and oxygen content too low for humans and Kzinti
Human Population:	About 8.5 million, spread out in comfortable high-density habitats and domed cities

DOWN

Down is the home world of the Grogs, disturbing aliens who possess heightened mind control abilities. Down once had a long-established Kzinti military outpost that maintained a fleet of Kzinti warships within easy striking distance of Earth's developing interstellar colonies.

Down was liberated after the fist Man-Kzin Wars. In present day, humans and Grogs work harmoniously in all fields of mutual interest, but Grogophobia is still prevalent.

History of Known Space — *The Guide to Larry Niven's Ringworld*

System:	L5 1668
Distance From Sol:	12.3 light years
Size:	14,700 Kilometers at the Equator Slightly larger than Earth
Surface Gravity:	1.15 gee
Day:	28.7 UNS Hours
Year:	67 UNS Days
Moons:	None
Distance From Primary:	13 Million Miles
Chief Industries:	Major fish farming industries run by Dolphins
Atmosphere:	Tranquil red-desert world with dusty but breathable air
Human Population:	About 360 million living in high-density wheeled space colonies in orbit around Down; some 30 million live on the surface in widely separated urban oases

HOME

Home has a strange history. First settled in 2189, the colonists thought they had discovered Eden. By the mid-24th century they had developed a healthy industrial civilization.

In 2351, the human protector Brennan modified the tree-of-life virus and turned the population of Home into protectors, who went off to fight the oncoming fleet of protectors from the galactic core. Everyone on Home disappeared. Kzinti were wrongly accused of having obliterated the Home colony. Kzinti legends describe horrible parasitic creatures that emerged from a cycle of deep slumber and devoured the colonists, but no evidence of such monsters has ever been found.

The planet was judged unsafe for human habitation for two centuries. Home was officially recolonized in 2589. Growth and development has proceeded cautiously.

System:	Epsilon Indi
Distance From Sol:	11.4 light years
Size:	14,129 Kilometers at the Equator Slightly larger than Earth
Surface Gravity:	1.08 gee
Day:	23.2 UNS Hours
Year:	181 UNS Days
Moons:	One

Distance From Primary:	**80 Million Miles**
Chief Industries:	**Extensive mining operations, farms, aquaculture**
Atmosphere:	**Earth-like**
Human Population:	**51 million**

JINX

Jinx is the largest, most technologically-advanced, and most highly-industrialized human colony world. Jinx is the major moon of the third planet from Sirius A, Binary, a banded orange gas giant more massive than Jupiter.

General Products maintains a major regional facility on Jinx and it is home to the Institute of Knowledge, the finest museum and research complex in human space. Since Jinx proclaimed itself independent of UN control in 2200, it has become an interstellar melting pot with alien populations sometimes equalling humans. Certain sections have gained reputations as safe havens for outlaws, smugglers, and pirates. The ARM maintains an outpost here per an agreement between the UN and Jinx to police alien relations.

System:	**Sirius A**
Distance From Sol:	**8.7 light years**
Size:	**Overall, small than Earth**
	Egg shaped with colorful bands, six times denser than Earth
Surface Gravity:	**1.78 gee**
Day:	**96 UNS Hours**
	The same face, the East End, is always turned to the gas giant planet, Binary
Year:	**About 453 UNS Days**
Moons:	**None**
Distance From Primary:	**397 Million Miles**
Chief Industries:	**High-technology and research, alien studies**
Atmosphere:	**Habitable Earth-like bands; bands of seas and lowlands are thick and dense with temperatures higher than 200 degrees F**
Human Population:	**Over 2.1 billion**

PLATEAU

In 2090 an Earth colony ship arrived at Tau Ceti following reports from an earlier ramrobot that one planet in the system was Earthlike. The closest they could find was a Venus type world with a poisonous, corrosive atmosphere lethal to humans. There would be no rescue and no escape. Finally the radar picked out what the ramrobot had found, a vast multi-plateaued mountain the size of California projecting above the deadly lower atmosphere. The atmosphere on the mountain was surprisingly Earthlike.

The pilot gasped, "Lookitthat!" christening the great peak forever.

Surrounding the great plateaus are spectacular waterfalls at the Void Edge. The colony quickly adapted to the mountainous environment and Lookitthat! became a panorama resembling old 20th century Europe. Many quaint mountain villages and resort towns spread about the various levels. Tourism is the major business. Fabulous resorts, casinos, and spas are major attractions perched high above the fabulous views over the Void's Edge.

System:	**Tau Ceti**
Distance From Sol:	**11.8 light years**
Size:	**12,309 Kilometers at the Equator Smaller than Earth, and less dense**
Surface Gravity:	**.81 gee**
Day:	**29.4 UNS Hours**
Year:	**241 UNS Days**
Moons:	**None**
Distance From Primary:	**100 Million Miles**
Chief Industries:	**Tourism**
Atmosphere:	**The plateaus of Mt. Lookitthat vary little in its pleasantly moderate climate and seasons. The rest of the planet is covered in swirling poisonous mist.**
Human Population:	**Permanent population is 105 million. Three orbital stations hold a million more.**

WE MADE IT

We Made It was settled when a ramrobot landed on a rare mild spring day near one of the planet's viscous, algae-chocked "oceans." After it reported favorable conditions, colonists arrived and found a planet whose odd axis of rotation cause perpetual daylight summers and winters of eternal night. Hurricane-force winds scour the surface throughout the year. The landscape is flat, utterly lifeless, sandblasted desert.

The colonists were nicknamed "crashlanders" and the struggle to build a civilization endured and developed underground. The savage power of the surface winds evolutionized the colonies into buried cities. Refineries for processing the rich algae oceans were developed. We Made Its severe isolation ended in 2410 when an Outsider merchant ship arrived and offered the sale of the Quantum I hyperdrive engine, resulting in a sudden industrial revolution.

System:	**Procyon**
Distance From Sol:	**11.3 light years**
Size:	**About 10,000 Kilometers at the Equator**
Surface Gravity:	**.59 gee**
Day:	**20.4 UNS Hours**
Year:	**853 UNS Days**
Moons:	**None**
Distance From Primary:	**195 Million Miles**
Chief Industries:	**Soft sciences, creative arts, synthetic food stuffs, manufacturing**
Atmosphere:	**Fairly dense, often dusty oxygen atmosphere**
Human Population:	**950 million**

WUNDERLAND

The first of the human interstellar colonies was established on a beautiful, idyllic, Earthlike world called Wunderland in 2091. Originally settled by elite, aristocratic families whose resources had financed the settlement, Wunderland's society is the closest thing to royalty in Human Space. City-states grow around the sites of magnificent estates, plantations, and baronial villas of the rich and powerful. Its infamy as the home to so much interstellar wealth has made Wunderland's history rife with political intrigue and conflict.

The Kzinti discovered Wunderland and conquered it in 2367, initiating the first Man-Kzin war. During the years of Kzinti occupation, the aristocracy suffered terribly, many becoming servants to the "ratcats" while others were were killed or eaten. Wunderland families maintain strong anti-Kzin alliances.

System:	**Alpha Centauri**
Distance From Sol:	**4.3 light years**
Size:	**9,780 Kilometers at the Equator Smaller than Earth**
Surface Gravity:	**.61 gee**
Day:	**26.7 UNS Hours**
Year:	**529 UNS Days**
Moons:	**None**
Distance From Primary:	**123 Million Miles**
Chief Industries:	**Farming, zero-gee manufacturing**
Atmosphere:	**Earth-like with pastoral and comfortable temperatures**
Human Population:	**3.25 billion**

THE BELT

Ceres, the largest asteroid, is the capital of the Belt. The rest of the asteroids are usually between one hundred meters to ten kilometers in diameter, made from ice, stone, and nickel. The most important product from the Belt is monopoles, which are used in fusion generators to create strong magnetic fields.

A phenomenon called the "Far Look" is a form of self-hypnosis that occurs when humans stare out too long into the infinite depths of space. The human loses all sense of time and self, and sometimes never returns to coherence; the Far Look claims the lives of many Belters.

MAJOR RACES OF KNOWN SPACE

28	THRINT AND TNUCTIPUN
33	PAK
46	PUPPETEERS
62	KZINTI

THRINT

Several billion years before the construction of Ringworld, a race known as the Thrint developed an irresistible telepathic ability called the Power, which made it easy for them to impose their will on other species. The Thrint enslaved all the intelligent organisms they encountered and used the technological skills of the slave races to build a vast interstellar empire spanning much of the Milky Way.

They became known as the Slavers.

A single Thrint family often owned and ruled an entire slave planet. Eventually, a slave race of advanced biological engineers, the Tnuctipun, found a way to rebel. They created the Bandersnatchi, a semi-sentient species immune to the Power and used them to help destroy the Slavers.

THE SLAVER WAR

In the war between the Slavers and the Tnuctipun, nearly all sentient races in the galaxy were destroyed. The Thrint used powerful thought-amplifiers to order their rebellious slave races to commit suicide. However, the Slaver Empire could not support its own weight without its workers; without slaves, the Thrint also perished.

All that remains of the vast Slaver empire, scattered through the spiral arms of the galaxy, were hundreds of primitive food planets, "seeded" with Tnuctipun-developed food-yeast. The yeast survived and mutated. Several billion years later, it evolved into terrestrial life on Earth, Pak life in the galactic core, and a variety of other advanced species–Puppeteer, Kzinti, Kdatlyno, and others in Known Space. It is no coincidence that carbon-based species are similar down to the molecular level on Earth, the Pak homeworld, and Ringworld. Millions of years ago, it was no accident that stargoing Protectors singled out Earth as a possible new Pak home because of the favorable conditions.

ESCAPING THE WAR

Thrint have been known to escape their extinction by encasing themselves in stasis fields, remaining alive in frozen time for billions of years. Any unlucky creature that happens to inadvertently release a Thrint would be in for a terrible surprise.

PHYSICAL DESCRIPTION

Thrint are squat, greenish humanoids with blocky torsos and stumpy legs. Their massive arms end in hands like three-fingered mechanical grabs. They have a neckless torso and a triangular hump behind the head. One single eye peers out from a vertical slit of a lid. Thick chicken-like claws form the footclaws. They have a thick hide that looks somewhat reptilian.

An obscene gash of mouth full of wet needle teeth is surrounded by bunched tendrils, like twenty wire worms or writhing tentacles. These eating tendrils surround the mouth and stroke caressingly at almost nonexistent lips.

A pointed tongue is used to groom the wormy tendrils.

A THRINT ORDERS ITS SLAVES TO SUICIDE

TNUCTIPUN

The Tnuctipun were an advanced race of biological engineers conquered by the Thrint billions of years ago. Most information about them comes from piecing together bits of history as related by the Bandersnatchi. Controlled for thousands of years as a slave race, these little aliens became incredibly hostile and paranoid, distrusting all other civilizations. They eventually led a rebellion against the Slavers and used their creations to destroy the Thrint. Before the Thrints' demise, the first of the slave races the Slavers commanded to suicide were the Tnuctipun.

Theorists speculate that some Tnuctipun may have escaped the death of their race in Slaver stasis fields, carrying with them powerful relics and devices of exotic high technology better left locked away.

DESCRIPTION

Tnuctipun stand about three feet tall. They are fairly humanoid with two arms and two squat legs. Their bodies have a cretaceous exoskeleton that gives excellent protection from the elements. They have four long tapered fingers on each hand with two opposable thumbs, well designed for precision engineering work.

The Tnuctipun knowledge of exotic weaponry, in addition to their innate hostility towards other aliens, makes them unpredictable and dangerous.

A TNUCTIP PREPARES ITSELF FOR THE LONG JOURNEY IN STASIS

"Suppose you could save the Ringworld by killing one and a half trillion inhabitants out of thirty trillion. A protector would do that, wouldn't she? Five percent to save 95 percent. It seems so…efficient."

The relationship of the Pak with the origins of man is profoundly disturbing. Humanity evolved from Pak children who once migrated to the Earth in search of suitable breeding grounds.

The Pak themselves are extremely intelligent, strong, and xenophobic. They developed space travel over three million years before the appearance of mankind and extensively exploited the asteroid belt and surrounding planets of systems near their homeworld.

Purity of the race is the primary Pak motivation. The Pak have never cooperated with other alien species; whenever they encounter other sentients, they destroy them as quickly and efficiently as possible to assure the purity of the Pak. No part of a destroyed alien culture is preserved.

THE PAK LIFE-CYCLE

The Pak native world is part of the galactic core, where stars form a spherical cloud about 7,000 light years in diameter. Their planet is slightly smaller than Earth with a lighter oxygen content mixed with 2% helium. The yellow-white G star sheds cool, green-tinged light onto a surface rich with strange, powerful smells. The soil of the Pak homeworld is rich in thallium oxide, an element not commonly found outside of worlds in the galactic core. Thallium oxide provides the key element that allows a bush called *tree-of-life* to propel Pak through their final and most important physiological transformation.

The Pak life cycle has three distinct stages: childhood, breeder, and protector. The first stage lasts from infancy to adolescence. Breeders are humanoids that resemble *Homo habilis* in physiology and development of the cranium. Their use of tools and language is minimal, and their memories are filled with nothing more than direct images of overpowering experiences, such as pain, fighting, and eating. A breeder's sole purpose is to create more children.

PROTECTORS

A breeder who survives to be 42 UNS years old gets the urge to gorge on the once-repugnant yam-like root of tree-of-life, which grows all over Pak. Tree-of-life has shiny green leaves, and its twisted pale-yellow roots look like yams or sweet potatoes. When a breeder eats the root, dramatic physiological and emotional changes occur, spurred on by the symbiotic virus which lives in tree-of-life (thallium oxide is required for the virus to live). The breeder metamorphoses into a protector, the last stage of the Pak cycle.

During the transformation, the breeder's skull softens and expands to accommodate an enlarged and more complex brain. A protective bony crest hardens on the skull, which has lost its forehead and chin. The eyes become set in deep pits beneath the jutting brow. The breeder's teeth fall out, and the gums and lips fuse together to form a flat "beak." All external sexual organs disappear, and a two-chamber heart develops in the groin from two large veins in the legs.

A protector's skin loses all its hair and becomes tough and leathery, enough armor to deflect a knife. Its joints swell, especially around the limbs, shoulders, and hips, giving greater leverage through an increased moment-arm. A protector's agility is increased by its newly acquired strength, which is enough to lift ten times its body mass.

The protector emerges from the transformation sharply sentient; its senses of touch, taste, and especially smell become hundreds of times more powerful than a breeder's. Its memories and experiences as a breeder crystallize into new clarity and a new sense of purpose.

Tree-of-life root is the protector's preferred food.

NOTES ON TREE-OF-LIFE

The amount of energy required for a breeder to transform into a protector is enormous. This must mean that tree-of-life root is high in energy-releasing nutrients. It is also likely that the symbiotic virus living in the root is capable of converting breeder cell tissue into protector tissue by burning these nutrients, forcing the mitochondria in the cells to increase their energy output, required to complete the transformation.

TREE-OF-LIFE GARDEN ON THE RINGWORLD

THE PROTECTOR COMPULSION

The protector quickly matures into an immensely powerful being, a ferocious and cunning warrior dedicated to one purpose: defend, protect, and expand the breeder population of its own bloodline at the expense of all other lines.

Every decision a protector makes is connected to the urge to protect its own bloodline. Protectors recognize members of their family clans most accurately by the correct smell. If a breeder smells wrong because of mutation, it is immediately destroyed by a family protector. This behavior provides a check on unacceptable mutation since radiation is heavy in the galactic core. However, this genetic imperative dooms all protectors to eternal warfare within and among themselves, and inhibits Pak expansion.

The Pak race can never be free of war. Protectors cannot cooperate amongst themselves unless they see a way to gain advantage over other protectors. The Pak's social progress is irrecoverably retarded by their genetic imperatives; knowledge and discoveries are often lost during the many wars that scar their history. When the Pak expand out to new worlds to find space for their breeders, the colonies are often destroyed by waves of ships from other protector families following years later.

CHILDLESS PROTECTORS

The advantages of a protector are out-balanced by the conflict between their vast intellect and inherited instincts. A protector's behavior is obviously dominated by overpowering internal tensions, and they maintain their mental stability in pursuit of external activity, all of which involve the advancement of their bloodlines. Protectors have no interest in art, luxury, or pure science.

A protector is not always in a state of warfare. If the breeders are safe, the protector can fall into a state of dreamlike lassitude. This is especially true of protectors whose "children" have been destroyed. However, the childless protector might remain in the dream state until it starves (though they live for thousands of years).

The only way for the protector to avoid this death is to find a new purpose. A childless protector can generalize the entire Pak species as its children, but then must find a useful way to advance the species. On occasion, the childless protector might journey to the great Pak library.

THE GREAT PAK LIBRARY

The records of uncountable interplanetary and interstellar flights are filed in the virtually indestructible books of the Pak library, located in a desert seeded with cobalt to ensure that protectors will not try to use the area as a breeder home. None of the Pak know who built the library, and its existence is an enigma since it seems that the protectors are unable to cooperate long enough to build such a structure.

The library is exclusively used and staffed by childless protectors, who have little to fear from other protectors since the building is located in a useless radioactive wasteland. A childless protector may read in the library for decades, playing a game with itself where its instincts tell it to enter the dream-state because there is no purpose in its living, and its vast intellect uses the convincing argument that as long as it is alive and reading in the library, its life has purpose.

The majority of the texts are about spaceflight, with the understanding that whatever contributes to the field will eventually allow the Pak to find a new home, a basic Pak assumption and drive. Other books are about space technology engineering, subnuclear physics, astronomy, gravitation, and ecology.

Despite their studies into these fields, the Pak science of space flight has never expanded beyond the use of relatively primitive interstellar ramjets and simple gravity polarizers. Since the Pak do not seek knowledge for its own sake, they never discovered hyperwave theory, the mathematical basis for hyperspace travel and communication. Ramjets and polarizers are the most scientifically "obvious" of all space technology developments.

THE GREAT PAK LIBRARY

Major Races of Known Space — *The Guide to Larry Niven's Ringworld*

THE PAK AND EARTH

One of the interstellar flight records in the Pak library tells of a group of childless protectors who intended to find a second homeworld for the Pak. They had planned to find a migration route into the spiral arms, where there were an abundance of yellow suns. They began their trip by carving out a huge nickel-iron asteroid, shaping the metals and stony strata to accommodate the equipment necessary for prolonged space travel, such as a life-support module and fuel-breeding nuclear pile.

The protectors exterminated the protectors of a large family, gaining control of the breeders. The breeders and seventy more childless protectors were put into a vast frozen-sleep chamber on board the asteroid-ship; two protectors remained as pilots. A selection of important life forms were also put into the frozen-sleep chamber.

The ship headed outward on a radial line from the galactic hub at 2% of the speed of light. The ship's ability to change course was extremely limited but they had no doubt they would travel a long time to find another Pak homeworld. The pilots found many systems with suitable yellow suns that might have been able to sustain Pak life, but the suns were too far off course.

The protectors began to die of old age, a phenomenon so intriguing that the information was beamed back to the Pak world. Half the protectors were dead after 500,000 years of travel, having been revived to pilot the ship. After 32,000 light years, the asteroid ship entered the solar system of Earth. They used the remainder of their fuel for braking and landing on the planet. Thirty protectors remained and nearly all of the breeders had survived.

Earth seemed ideal. The breeders were happy, turned loose in the forests and fields. The atmosphere and soil seemed safe, and any threatening indigenous life forms were exterminated. The protectors planted crops, dug mines, and created machines to do their work for them. They did not feel the urge to stop eating since there was so much work. They had no doubt that Earth would be the new Pak homeworld.

However, something was wrong with the tree-of-life gardens. Everything seemed fine except that the root did not transform breeders into protectors. The protectors assumed the root's fault had something to do with missing wavelengths of light from the sun. They never discovered that the problem was the lack of thallium oxide in the soil which allowed the symbiotic virus to grow.

Instead of attempting to refuel the ship in the vain hopes of finding another world to colonize, the protectors built a huge message laser and sent news of their plight back to Pak.

They asked for help and then died.

THE DEVELOPMENT OF MAN

The breeder population flourished even after the protectors died. The breeders evolved outside the constraints of Pak culture and the extreme radiation of the galactic core. However, the normal radiation from Earth's sun, in addition to normal cosmic background energies, mutated the breeders into the beginnings of modern man.

The physiological changes of a human's middle age are remnants from ancient Pak origins, but man merely grows old and dies without the additional genetic information provided by the tree-of-life root virus. Everything from the swelling of arthritis to loss of hair and teeth are part of the original process of becoming a protector. Only a "restlessness" remains, for tree-of-life.

HUMAN PROTECTORS

Humans as young as twenty UNS years are still vulnerable to the compulsion of tree-of-life. The scent of tree-of-life is irresistible, impelling the receiver to gorge on the root, overpowering all other considerations. Only the will of a reformed wirehead can resist the urge. Any person too old to eat the root dies in convulsions. Many people in the acceptable range of ages also die during the transformation, which might take weeks.

A human who survives the change becomes a human protector, differing from Pak protectors in a number of significant ways. Human protectors are not as strong or agile as Pak protectors, but they are much smarter and learn faster. Their thinking is much more flexible and they are less likely to commit themselves to irrevocable decisions.

The greatest difference in a human protector is the effect of personality on the actions of the protector. Most human protectors have a heightened aesthetic sense and sense of humor, and enjoy playing complex games and engaging in philosophical speculations. Love known from the previous life can also affect a human protector's judgement.

Human protectors are not as strongly motivated by genetic imperatives, and are often able to empathize with other sentient beings. They are not as xenophobic and often respect alien viewpoints. Boredom and the need for distraction are common human protector problems.

On occasion, a human protector might even admit a mistake.

PHSSTHPOK AND BRENNAN

The first Pak was encountered by humanity in 2125 when an interstellar fusion-ramship decelerated into the solar system. The ship was piloted by a childless protector named Phssthpok. While reading in the Pak library, Phssthpok had discovered an ancient message sent by a legendary Pak colony lost in the galactic arms. He instantly decided that he would find that world and save the colony of breeders. He traveled alone over 32,000 light years, over 1200 years, and found the Sol system.

The protector's fusion ramship was met by belter Jack Brennan. The belters had always hoped to meet an "outsider," believing that first contact would be friendly and beneficial. Instead of a friendly encounter, Phssthpok captured Brennan and fed him tree-of-life root as an experiment.

Brennan metamorphosed into the first human protector. Brennan immediately killed Phssthpok, realizing that the Pak would soon discover that the lost population of breeders had mutated in the two million year interval. Brennan knew that Phssthpok would have tried to exterminate the entire human race, in addition to sending a message back to the Pak homeworld.

Brennan took the Pak protector's ship and moved into the Oort cloud of the solar system to watch over and protect humanity. The belter prepared for eventual war with the Pak by building a better fusion ramship and developing gravity generation techniques.

Checking Phssthpok's logs, Brennan discovered that the first scouts of the Pak fleet were going to be near Epsilon Indi where the colony of Home was settled, 11.4 light years from Earth. He destroyed the scouts, then employed one of his descendants to expose the entire population of the colony to a clinically created strain of tree-of-life virus. The fraction who survived the transformation became human protectors. They left Home to fight the Pak ships traveling along Phssthpok's route.

The mummified remains of Phssthpok are kept in the Smithsonian Institute, along with the holographic records of Brennan's lectures concerning the origins of humanity and the threat of the Pak. Among Brennan's gifts to his children was the alleviation of the social problems caused by organ banks. The two centuries under his influence and aegis are remembered as a golden age on Earth.

THE PAK AND RINGWORLD

It is known that the Pak once lived on Ringworld; Ringworld is an ideal Pak breeding park. It is now believed the Pak did not build Ringworld originally, but merely discovered it and populated it with breeders, perhaps by an ancient Pak fleet tracing the path of the lost breeder colony on Earth.

The Pak protectors were exterminated quickly after their arrival. A mysterious disease killed them. It is speculated that one protector faction may have developed a genetic virus which doomed them all. Others speculate that the extermination of the Pak resulted from early business negotiations between the Puppeteers and the Outsiders.

After the protectors died, variant breeders evolved quickly and hominids multiplied, filling in every gap in the immense biological spectrum of the ring. The hominids flourished and progressed, evolving in ways no human could possibly imagine. On present day Ringworld, there are over a thousand distinct hominid types including predators, scavengers, ghouls, vampires, swamp-dwellers, and many more.

Pak tree-of-life gardens still exist on Ringworld, hidden in Pak mini-worlds. From time to time, one of Ringworld's hominid denizens may stumble upon tree-of-life root and survive the protector change. It is even possible that a massive dose of the Ringworld longevity drug (extracted from tree-of-life by City Builders) could trigger the transformation. These protectors have given rise over the years to legends of mighty, armored magicians who are awesome fighters, granting the gift of immortality or the gift of death, sometimes to entire races.

Hominid protectors share many of the characteristics of their Pak counterparts, such as increased strength, agility, and intelligence. Like humans, the characteristics of a race determine the actions and attitudes of these protectors. Different points of view, motivations, and moralities are the most common differences, reflecting the species' origins and place in the Ringworld environment.

THE HOMEWORLD PAK

The chain of explosions in the galaxy's core ended nearly 9,000 years ago. The density of the core, the geometry of the outburst, and the direction of its spread could contribute to the chances of the homeworld Pak's survival. The protectors could have easily anticipated the explosion and created huge fleets to transport the breeders to suitable worlds, as with the lost Earth colony.

A CHILDLESS PROTECTOR STUDIES VIGILANTLY IN THE PAK LIBRARY

Major Races of Known Space   The Guide to Larry Niven's Ringworld

PUPPETEERS

"You caused all this," said Louis Wu, "with your monstrous egotism…How could you be so powerful, so determined, and so stupid…"

Pierson's Puppeteers (first discovered by spacer Olaf Pierson) are a supra-intelligent species whose herd-beast ancestors only found solace and protection amongst their own kind. They were prey to many different carnivores, and for protection developed a disproportionate instinct for survival. This survival instinct did not take the form of overt aggressiveness, as was the case of the Kzinti, but appears as a racial trait that causes them to flee from danger in any form, no matter how insignificant or long-reaching in terms of the Puppeteers' advancement of their civilization. This instinct is often seen as over-cautiousness by humans and sheer cowardice by the Kzinti. As the Puppeteers developed, they were able to out-think the dangers of their homeworld, eventually becoming the dominant life-form. Puppeteer civilization rose long before the evolution of man on Earth.

The instincts of the Puppeteers force them to strive for dominance in the social orders of other races to ensure their own safety. They possess technology far in advance of any race (with the exception of the Outsiders), and have used this advantage as a means of indirect influence; the need for caution does not allow the Puppeteers to act directly with or against another race. They distrust aliens and the motives of aliens, conducting their business through agents or robotic intermediaries. As a result, the Puppeteer business empire filled ten million cubic light years, reaching civilizations unheard of by Known Space.

THE MADNESS OF THE PUPPETEERS

Puppeteers judge others of their race in terms of sanity. Sane Puppeteers have no need for variety or adventure, and never need to explore new territories of any sort on their own. They find no need for independence and, almost without exception, will only socialize with other Puppeteers.

Wishful thinking, superstition, and other predominantly human traits are completely alien to sane Puppeteers. They view humanity's discovery of scientific laws and alien worlds through trial-and-error, risk, and serendipity to be the height of imprudent thinking. The Puppeteers employ nothing but careful observation, investigation, and nearly unending experiments to ensure that no personal or social risk is taken by any portion of the race. Their powers of deductive reasoning and logic are unmatched.

The Puppeteers have a practical attitude toward problem

solving which is a reflection of their survival instinct; any act they perform (even on a personal level) is undoubtedly geared toward the safety of the race. Any act that conflicts with this basic instinct is considered insane. It is for this reason that the few Puppeteers who have had contact with other races are judged mad by their civilization, who see direct association with anything as dangerous and unpredictable as an alien an unreasonable risk.

PUPPETEER PRAGMATISM

The Puppeteers see no line between pragmatism and their safety. They are quite willing to go to any lengths to protect themselves and provide a safer environment, even if it means destroying another race. Their lack of moral sense could easily be construed as a ruthlessness matched only by warrior races like the Kzinti and Pak. The Puppeteers can be egotistical, manipulative, and arrogant to the point where they are blind to their own mistakes.

Puppeteers always assure themselves the advantage in interstellar affairs. To maintain their safety, they do not hesitate to resort to blackmail, bribery, or any other form of influence including carefully applied violence, though they would always hire an outside agency to perform such a task.

It is important to note that these practices of influence were easily incorporated into humanity's legal system.

PUPPETEER APPEARANCE

Most races in Known Space have similar exterior physiologies. The Puppeteers do not match this standard in any form; their appearance is shocking to most humans. Unlike other species, the Puppeteers strongly resemble the herd animals of their ancestry, a triangular body that is wider in the front than in the rear. Three legs end in small, pointed hooves set in a nearly perfect equilateral triangle. The skin is covered with a creamy-white hide, soft, and pleasant to touch.

A Puppeteer's mane-covered frontal hump is a thick, bony skull which protects its huge brain. Two independently working heads rise sinuously on flexible necks from either side of the braincase hump. The heads appear similar to the head of a python, including the snake's forked tongue. However, the Puppeteer's heads have dry, thick lips which extend several inches beyond the

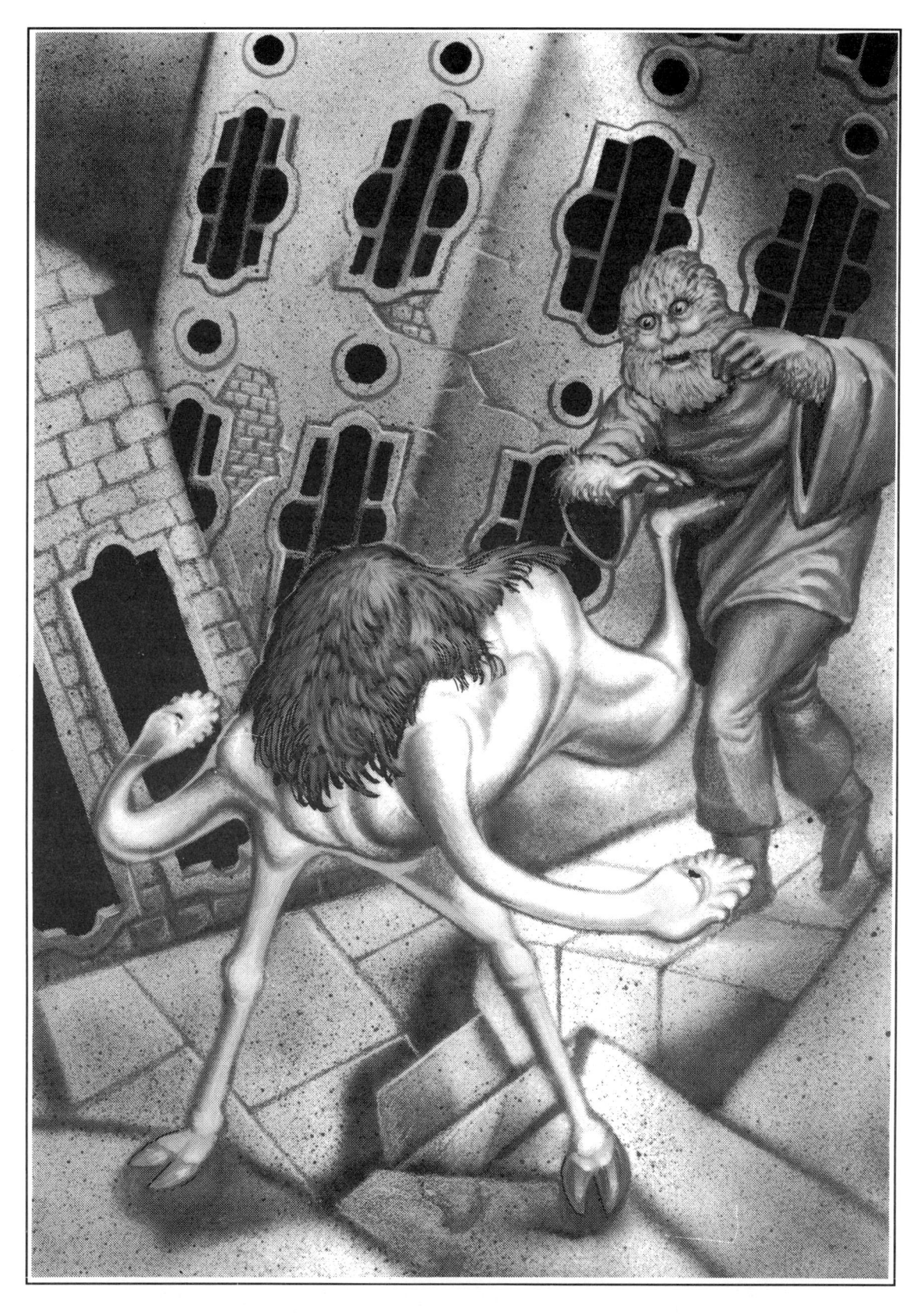

THE PUPPETEER DEFENSE MECHANISM

Major Races of Known Space — *The Guide to Larry Niven's Ringworld*

mouth, ending in fingerlike knobs. The Puppeteer uses the lips like hands, but with far more dexterity than any human; this is one of the reasons for the race's superior toolmaking. The forked tongue also serves as additional fingers.

Each head has one eye set deep in a protective socket of bone. Because the necks of the heads are capable of twisting in any direction, a Puppeteer has nearly perfect 360° vision (one head facing forward, the other facing back). A running Puppeteer holds one head high and the other low to obtain panoramic perception and to see around obstacles. The two heads also provide outstanding facility for precision work, since the Puppeteer has both a simultaneous close-up and general view of an operation.

In addition to their striking appearance, one of the most disturbing aspects of the Puppeteers (at least to a human) is the tendency of the heads to regard one another in silence or carry on conversations with themselves. A Puppeteer many also carry on two conversations at once. It is thought that the silent heads may be a form of Puppeteer laughter.

The hind leg is set in a complex hip joint, providing a range of complex motions. When a Puppeteer feels threatened, it defends itself by turning, facing both heads backwards, and kicking. A kick from a Puppeteer can easily kill a man outright. Coincidentally, it is this attack which has illuminated study of the Puppeteers, showing that the race does not run from danger, but instinctively turns *away* from danger, to turn and kick. The few Puppeteers questioned on this point say that sane Puppeteers always turn and run from danger, and add that the majority always judges what is sane and what is not.

GROOMING

Despite their strangeness of their appearance, most humans find sane Puppeteers beautiful to behold. A sane Puppeteer's mane is always well groomed, specially cut depending on social status and personal preference. Natural mane colors are similar to terrestrial horses, running from browns to auburn and yellows.

Puppeteers of high rank often ornament their manes with jewels or braid them with bright metallic strands. The manes themselves are kept fluffed, curled into ringlets, or straight. Their creamy hides practically glow.

A SANE PUPPETEER

Major Races of Known Space / The Guide to Larry Niven's Ringworld

Unkempt manes usually indicate insanity. The vanity of sane Puppeteers must create tremendous social pressure for the insane to keep well groomed, which most likely adds to the already existing insanity.

PUPPETEER LANGUAGE

The beautiful language of the Puppeteers cannot be imitated by beings with a single throat (which unfortunately includes every other sentient life-form in Known Space). The language's complexity is compounded by an eighteen note octave scale which apparently relates as much information to a Puppeteer as actual words. Their separate larynxes can produce intonations that range from dissonant harmonies to bursts of orchestral music. It is impossible to determine the sex of a Puppeteer by the timbre of its voice, and it is frustratingly thought by some male humans that the voice of a Puppeteer is that of an attractive woman.

The Puppeteers' huge brain allows them to carry on two independent conversations at the same time, in two separate languages. They are outstanding linguists, a feature of both their vast intelligence and their need to protect themselves diplomatically. They speak Interworld, the language of Known Space, when speaking to humans.

An upset Puppeteer loses the ability to maintain human vocal expression. A terrified Puppeteer's scream resembles a dying steam calliope.

SEX LIFE

Puppeteers do not discuss their sex life with aliens.

PUPPETEER MANIC-DEPRESSIVE CYCLE

In human terms, Puppeteers are egotistical, arrogant, and have no moral sense whatsoever. Puppeteers do not see this behavior as negative since the only thing that matters to them is their safety. A human sees a Puppeteer's behavior as deviant, but the only deviant behavior acknowledged by the Puppeteers themselves is their manic-depressive cycle.

All Puppeteers display this behavior. The manic-depressive cycle is triggered by shock or threat, either of mission failure or

AN INSANE PUPPETEER DISPLAYING PRUDENT BEHAVIOR

Major Races of Known Space

The Guide to Larry Niven's Ringworld

physical trauma. A depressed Puppeteer tucks both necks beneath its forelegs, folding itself into a catatonic, misshapen ball. The Puppeteer often remains folded for hours or possibly days, quivering with fear, withdrawn from a hostile universe. However, the presence of preventable danger often brings the Puppeteer out from hiding, giving way to unusual bouts of daring and heroism when the insanity of others makes no risk seem insane.

PUPPETEER POLITICS AND THE HINDMOST

The Puppeteer herd instinct of survival and protection influences every aspect of their lives. Their "turn from danger" instinct gives them a view that leadership is best provided from the rear, the area of greatest safety and wisdom. The supreme executive of Puppeteer government is called the Hindmost, or "he-who-leads-from-behind." Hindmost is also a term provided to the leader of any Puppeteer group or expedition.

The current Hindmost has a strong personality, unlike the majority of the Puppeteer race, who act strongly only when they perceive a danger that can be avoided and have a means to force aliens under their command to act. This is typically the case with manic-depressive Puppeteer emissaries. The Hindmost's actions are often unpredictable.

CONSERVATIVES VERSUS EXPERIMENTALISTS

Puppeteers have two different and nearly contradictory views about the direction their race's leadership should take: the Conservative and the Experimentalists. The Conservatives are unimaginative and cautious, believing that the Puppeteers must remain unknown by other alien races to maintain their safety.

The Experimentalists usually take power when some crisis threatens the Puppeteer race, such as the advance of the Kzinti empire or the discovery of the galactic core explosion. The Conservatives maintain their rule longer than the Experimentalists, who are usually deposed once they have acted and eliminated the threat.

The two factions have the safety of the Puppeteer race in mind, but have different solutions, one believing in noninterference, the other total control. The factions constantly bicker as to the guidance of the race's destiny.

HISTORY AND POLITICS

It is theorized by Known Space scientists that the greatest problem faced by any advancing civilization is not economics, health, or safety, but heat. Heat is produced by any sufficiently industrialized race in great amounts, and eventually the heat threatens the ecology of the planet, which in turn threatens the lives of everything on the world. Expansion to other systems is not a solution since the heat problems are merely carried from world to world.

The Puppeteers faced this dilemma early in their star-faring history. A Conservative faction ruled at the time, and they were forced to hear insane proposals from the Experimentalists. The Conservatives relinquished control of the seat of government to the other party. The Puppeteer homeworld was moved away from its sun to dissipate the heat, and four farming worlds were terraformed, seeded, and placed in convenient orbits.

The Puppeteer planet had escaped its danger. The Experimentalists were immediately removed from power by the Conservatives, who maintained control for centuries. However, the Experimentalists were still a strong force in Puppeteer government and took control for brief periods to expand the commercial interests of their financial empire. The General Products Corporation was formed by the Experimentalists to allow the Puppeteers control over the advance of alien races and as a medium for initial contact.

The Kzinti threat brought the Experimentalists back to power after six centuries. It was their monumental egotism that influenced the development of both mankind and the Kzinti Patriarchy during the Man-Kzin Wars. The Experimentalists ensured that the humans would be able to buy an Outsider hyperdrive shunt, ensuring military disaster for the Kzinti and killing four generations of aggressive Kzinti warriors; this left more tractable Kzinti to breed and control the government.

The General Products Corporation gained enormous profit from trade with Known Space. It was at this point that the Experimentalists began directly manipulating the destiny of man.

THE BIRTHRIGHT LOTTERIES AND PSYCHIC LUCK

The history of mankind is littered with near-misses and escapes that could easily have spelled disaster for the entire race.

Nuclear war was a constant threat for many years, while pollution, corruption, and economic difficulties were capable of laying waste to the population in ways more subtle but equally absolute.

According to the Puppeteers, luck is the strongest and most desirable trait in humans. The Experimentalists began a plan to systematically breed humans for luck through bribery and blackmail of the officials in charge of Earth's fertility laws, created to reduce overpopulation. The law stated that parents could not have more than one child, and some people could have none depending on genetic defect or aberrant behavior; however, the Birthright Lotteries allowed some to have multiple children, as many as they wanted for every Lottery won.

The Puppeteer Experimentalists believed that one way to win the Birthright Lottery was through luck. They selected sixth generation Lottery winners for the experiment in the hopes that their luck would "rub off" on Nessus, the Puppeteer who led the first expedition to the Ringworld, and shield him from danger.

The experiment was a resounding failure.

The effect of the Puppeteer interference in the Birthright Lotteries is only known by a select few humans and Kzinti, as is the reason for the Outsider sale of the hyperdrive to humanity, a related incident of luck. When questioned, the Puppeteers say they have saved humanity from enslavement, and the creation of less hostile Kzinti makes their extermination unnecessary.

Things were going very well for the Puppeteers until the discovery of the core explosion in the mid 2600s.

THE CORE EXPLOSION AND THE PUPPETEER MIGRATION

The nuclear forces within the core of the galaxy are tremendous and unstable. When a sun flares or goes nova, there is a chance that other suns will also be affected, flaring or going nova. The Puppeteers hired Beowulf Shaeffer, a human scout pilot, to use the first Quantum II hyperdrive ship and investigate new readings from the galactic core.

Shaeffer discovered that the core had undergone a cataclysmic explosion, and the radiation shockwave was going to reach Known Space in 20,000 years. The Puppeteers immediately panicked in fear of the "impending" disaster; the Experimentalists came to power at once to orchestrate the extragalactic migration.

They bought a drive from the Outsiders capable of moving the Puppeteer worlds through space at near-light speeds rather than risk hyperspace migration. The five worlds are arrayed in the stable pattern of a Kemplerer rosette, heading toward the Lesser Magellanic Cloud 200,000 light years away. Artificial suns keep the four farming worlds' plants alive, while the last world is solely lit by the lights of its streets and industry.

A few humans have been allowed to settle on one of the farming worlds. Conservatives use the humans to investigate dangerous regions in the path of the migration.

The Puppeteers vanished entirely with the exception of a handful of courageously insane, mainly left behind to handle unfinished business and to keep an eye on developments in Known Space.

THE EXPERIMENTALISTS AFTER THE MIGRATION

The Experimentalists believe they have chosen the safest possible method of travel. Flying five worlds through space is dangerous. The unknown depths of the intergalactic void could hold terrifying surprises.

Once the exodus was under way, the Experimentalists were deposed and the Conservatives took power. The Conservatives want nothing more to do with the Ringworld. Experimentalist factions have their doubts; they believe it will take approximately 87,000 years relative time (180,000 light-years) to make the journey. The Fleet isn't efficient enough to maintain itself that long without outside resources. The Experimentalists believe that the Puppeteers will have to migrate to a new home, and the Ringworld would be an excellent choice. The Ringworld could even serve as a refugee ship.

The Experimentalists are also determined to learn who built the Ringworld. They feel it would be important for them to know if there is a need to defend the Puppeteer race against the Ringworld Engineers.

GENERAL PRODUCTS CORPORATION

Though many of their engineering secrets were bought from the Outsiders, the Puppeteers have the most advanced science in Known Space. The General Products Corporation was created by the Puppeteers to trade and sell alien goods with other species.

THE PUPPETEER FLEET-OF-WORLDS

Direct contact with humans did not begin until the latter portion of the 25th century, after the First Man-Kzin War. The Outsider hyperdrive which ended the war also gave mankind the ability to explore surrounding systems and end the vulnerable isolation of established colonies. There was a huge market for safer spaceships, which the Puppeteers were expert at providing. The Puppeteers established offices on Jinx and We Made It, and by the mid-2600s, the General Product Corporation employed over two billion humans.

The Puppeteers' sudden departure from Known Space caused a stock market crash that almost ended humanity's interstellar trade.

Despite the disappearance of their empire, Puppeteer products continue to revolutionize the technology of Human Space.

PUPPETEER TECHNOLOGY

The caution of the Puppeteers makes them unwilling to use any products but their own. The reliability of General Products Corporation drive systems, stasis fields, and other items, combined with the Puppeteer's reputation of universal cowardice, has made other races share that faith.

All Puppeteer artifacts share the same features of design. Furniture, weapons, and tools are perfectly smooth, as if made of frozen mercury; there are no sharp edges or corners. All work with unobtrusive perfection and are equally expensive, but worth the additional cost.

The creations of the Puppeteers are often multifunctional to the point where the user feels there is a deliberate attempt to hide more dangerous features. For instance, the flashlight laser can be used as a normal electric torch or as a deadly weapon. The Puppeteer disintegrator has a double aperture, one for suppressing the negative charge of an atom, the other the positive; when both barrels are used, an electric arc creates a powerful explosion. The caution of the Puppeteers' does not allow the race to believe such "additional features" are weapons, as they always avoid anything dangerous. However, if someone in their employ finds a lethal use for a harmless device, especially as a means to provide the Puppeteer with protection, then that just means the device is better designed than planned.

Or so it is said.

The Puppeteers use four different types of superconductors, only two of which are known to humans and Kzinti, and only one of which is susceptible to the superconductor plague launched against Ringworld. They have not sold the secret of the other two superconductors to any party in Known Space. The Puppeteers also employ light bending and sonic suppression fields in their homeworld urban parks to isolate them from the rest of busy Puppeteer society.

Puppeteers have the ability to track ships in hyperspace and communicate through hyperpulse in a gravity well, two feats which baffle Known Space scientists. It is suspected the Puppeteers bought these two items of technology from the Outsiders to assist in the second exploration of the Ringworld. In addition, the Puppeteers also have more advanced thrusting systems which can sustain higher accelerations than those units carried by Known Space ships.

Earth uses teleportation booths to provide near-instantaneous travel throughout the world, but the Puppeteers have created a series of stepping disks which allow them instant travel; they can walk the entirety of their homeworld in minutes, giving them "seven league boots." Unlike the booths, the stepping disks can be installed anywhere and are portable. The General Products Corporation has the rights to manufacture and sell Pelton transfer booths, but have never offered to sell the secret of the stepping disk.

Though the Puppeteers make invulnerable spaceship hulls, they refuse to equip warships.

THE SUPERCONDUCTOR PLAGUE

The Outsiders sold the Puppeteers the location of the Ringworld in 1733 a.d. Searching for a way to expand trade at no risk, the Experimentalists immediately sent robotic probes to determine the feasibility of an expedition.

The Puppeteers mistook the City Builders to be the Ringworld's engineers and become suddenly afraid to encounter so powerful a race. The Puppeteers examined the Ringworld's superconductor material and created a technophytic bacterium to seed the Ringworld and destroy the superconductor. The strategy was to follow the probes with trading ships and come to the profitable rescue of the City Builders. However, the Puppeteers quickly realized that the City Builders could not have possibly created the Ringworld, and soon discovered several Pak artifacts. The Puppeteers feared the Pak above nearly all other threats.

The Conservatives took control of the government and the Ringworld was abandoned. The Experimentalists regained power under the threat of Kzinti expansion and decided that a manned expedition to the Ringworld might reveal treasures worth the risk (especially if they could convince others to take the risk for them). When the decision was made, the plague had reduced the Ringworld to barbarism, destroying thousands of years of civilization.

It is unknown if a new strain of the superconductor bacterium still survives on the Ringworld.

KZINTI

"For several hundred years, the fittest of your species were those members with the wit or the forbearance to avoid fighting human beings. For nearly two hundred kzin years there has been peace between man and kzin."

"But there would be no point! We could not win a war!"

"That did not stop your ancestors."

The Kzinti's earliest ancestors were plains cats, and they have lost none of that animal's inherent ferocity during their evolution. They remain carnivorous, impatient, aggressive, and unreasonably impulsive, but also have developed an uncompromising sense of personal honor, courage, and duty; it is said by the Kzinti themselves that if honor requires a Kzin to starve while within reach of meat, then he will starve.

Aggressiveness and the belief in domination of the weak has convinced the Kzinti that their ultimate role is to rule (at minimum) the entire galaxy. They built an empire over thousands of years which was so vast that it covered three times the area of Known Space. Many sentient species who desired peaceful contact and trade become Kzinti slaves and meat animals.

The Kdatlyno were discovered after they attempted to use the 21-centimeter interstellar hydrogen radio band to contact other intelligent life-forms. Interstellar radio is filled with the sounds of stars. The 21-centimeter band is remarkably silent, cleaned for use by countless cubic light years of cold interstellar hydrogen. It is the natural line for any intelligent race to use in attempts to contact another race. The Kzinti detected the Kdatlyno, correctly guessed that the race would have valuable resources, and immediately dispatched a fleet.

The worlds of conquered aliens become colonies and forward bases. The Kzinti Empire was able to further expand its borders with these new planetary resources and stolen technologies.

Fortunately, the Kzinti expansion was stopped before they enslaved the Earth.

THE MAN-KZIN WARS

The Kzinti drive for conquest makes them implacable foes. Their formidable warships plied the light years until they met the first fusion ramships of Earth, ending Earth's golden age of space exploration that had lasted over two centuries.

The Kzinti ships used the gravity polarizer, which allowed their dreadnoughts short, sustained bursts of incredible speed. This made them infinitely more maneuverable than the fusion ramships and had the occasional effect of terrifying the overwhelmed human crews.

Earth had not known a war since the age of exploration began and none of the ships carried armaments; as it had been assumed that first contact with an alien race would be friendly. There was no warfleet to protect the Centauri system from the single Kzinti Conqueror-class warship that took Wunderland for the Kzin Patriarchy.

THE KZINTI LESSON

In the early days of the war, the human crews created makeshift weapons, like the infamous "galactic grenade," which was nothing more than a barrel filled with ball bearings and fitted with a radio detonator. When the barrel reached an enemy warship, the detonator shot the bearings away with such force that they could penetrate a hull. Unfortunately, there were many simple ways to shield a ship from micrometeors that were also effective against the steel bearings, and the bearings sometimes found their way back to the Earth ships.

Despite their obvious superiority in technology, the Kzinti always attacked before they were properly prepared, impatient to sweep through systems for personal honor and the honor of the empire. The resistance from Earth should have been minimal and ineffective except that, historically speaking, humans are the most resourceful when they have nothing left to lose.

Early interstellar ramships employed fusion-powered photon drives. The ships were launched by photon sails and the laser cannon batteries on the asteroids. The cannons were fired into the sails, providing the ramships with initial motive power before their huge scoops could pick up enough interstellar hydrogen to begin the fusion process. When the Kzinti ships moved within range of the cannons, the humans crews fired and tore the enemy apart.

The Kzinti Lesson is, "a reaction drive's efficiency as a weapon is in direct proportion to its efficiency as a drive."

The Kzinti campaign against the Solar System ended with terrible losses for the Kzinti. The Kzinti telepaths had accurately reported that Earth had no weapons, but the resourceful humans had found other means to combat the enemy.

However, the Kzinti still held the superiority in numbers, technology, and experience. The war was slowed by the unexpected resistance and the lightspeed barrier that prevented ships from quickly covering the distances between the worlds. The war lasted for decades and humanity would have lost eventually, had the Puppeteers not interfered.

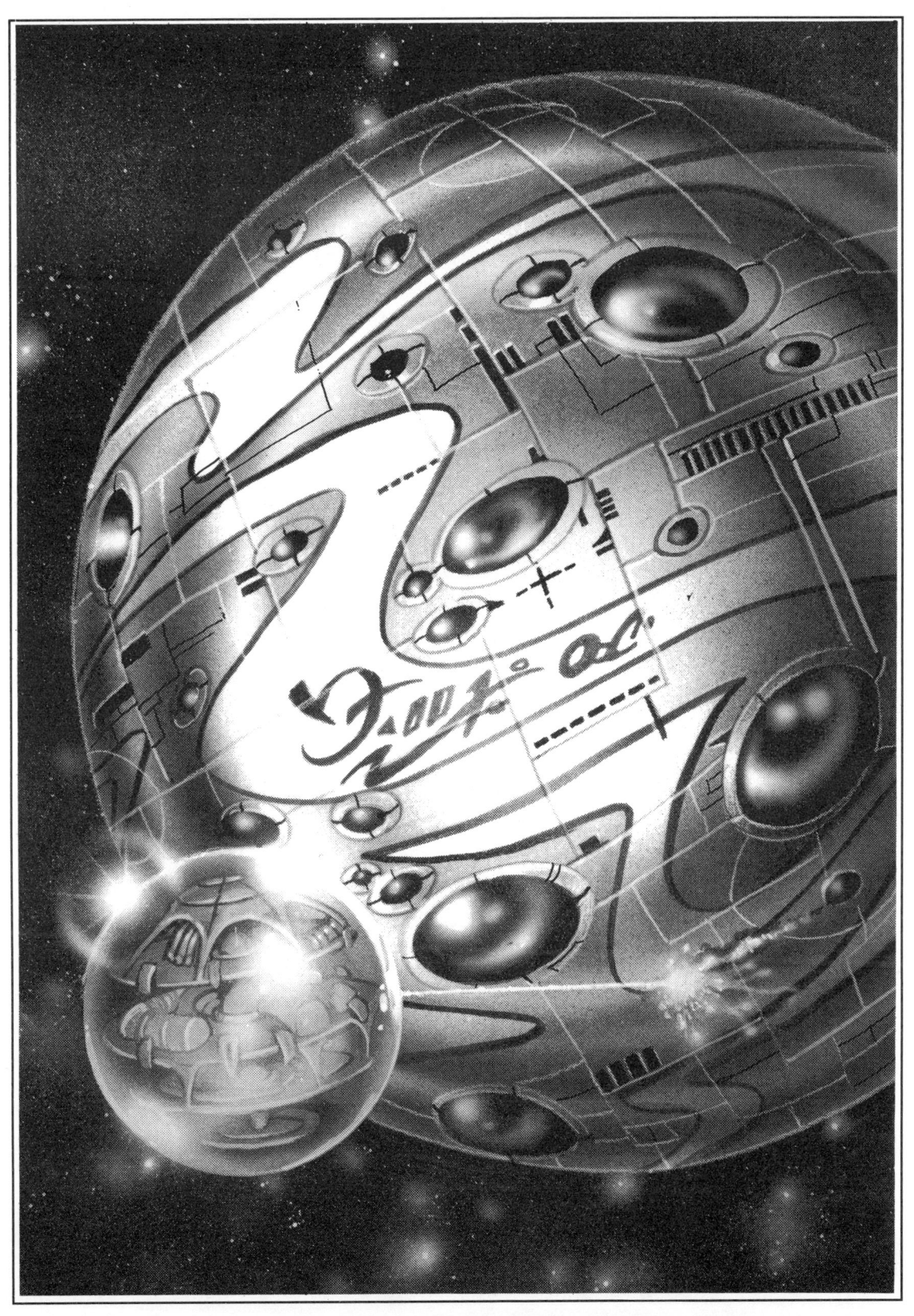

*THE FIRST QUANTUM I HYPERDRIVE SHIP ATTACKS
AN **IMPERIAL CONQUEROR** CLASS DREADNOUGHT*

Major Races of Known Space   *The Guide to Larry Niven's Ringworld*

THE PUPPETEERS' INFLUENCE ON THE MAN-KZIN WARS

With their proverbial caution, the Puppeteers studied the Kzinti carefully for hundreds of years. The Kzinti were a dangerous race who would no doubt attempt to take the Puppeteer homeworld and make slaves of the inhabitants. Though there was no possibility for the relatively unsophisticated Kzinti to achieve such a goal, the Puppeteers were unwilling to give them the chance. They created a plan to exterminate the entire Kzinti race and were ready to begin implementation when the first Man-Kzin war provided an alternate solution.

The solution first involved a great deal of debating over the threat of the Kzinti. Experimentalist factions said that the Kzinti might provide a useful buffer against possible attacks from other races, such as the Pak, or whoever constructed the Ringworld. Conservative factions argued that the race should be exterminated simply because they were too dangerous for a comfortable margin of Puppeteer safety. The Experimentalists were coming into power at the time of the debates and their arguments prevailed. The result of the decision was to conduct a selective breeding experiment that would produce Kzinti who would be more docile and open to negotiations and politicking rather than open fighting.

The Kzinti ships were better armed and more maneuverable than the Earth fusion ramships, but the Puppeteers figured that giving the humans superior technology would undoubtedly kill the first generation of warriors from the Kzinti populace. The Puppeteers used a starseed lure to draw an Outsider ship into Human Space, where the mysterious race sold the mayor of the planet We Made It the secret of the Quantum I hyperdrive shunt (on credit).

The effect was immediate. The Kzinti ships could never hope to outdistance or catch a hyperdrive-equipped vessel. The war instantly turned against them and they were pushed back, planet by planet. As predicted by the Puppeteers, the most fierce and dangerous Kzinti were killed, assuring their stock would not breed again.

Defeat was not an idea taken well by the Kzinti, and revenge had always been a strong motivator for their race. The Kzinti restaged their attack against the human-held planets in the Second Man-Kzin War. Of course, the humans had learned their hard lesson. General Products hulls and thrusters significantly improved the human defensive fleet. No. 2 hulls were often converted from their original use as survey ships to attack vessels, while the huge

No. 3 hulls were made into battle cruisers equipped with reactionless thrusters, fusion drives, and the Quantum I hyperdrive. The Kzinti ran straight into Earth's new warships and quickly collapsed. Several of the Kzinti hold-worlds were annexed and the slave populations released.

The Kzinti were not willing to let another defeat go unpunished. They attacked again and were repulsed more easily. They attacked a fourth time, lost, and finally gave up, the empire they had built over thousands of years drastically reduced.

In each attack over the centuries, Kzin had lost two-thirds of its fighting population and was unable to recover its original fighting spirit. The population of the non-sentient females had been untouched by the ravages of the war and the Kzinti's numbers grew again, aggressive, but not dangerous enough for the Puppeteers to feel the race required extermination.

The Kzinti reluctantly opened diplomatic relations with other species.

THE PATRIARCHY

The Kzin social structure is similar to feudal Europe on Earth. The ruler of the empire is called the Patriarch, and he is the final arbitrator on all matters concerning the Patriarchy. Other hereditary names act like heraldry, identifying levels of nobility equivalent to dukes, barons, and similar grades. The current ruling family bears the *Riit* suffix at the end of their name.

Unlike Earthly feudal aristocracy, any Kzinti can earn a name. The current Patriarch did not earn his title through great deeds (though his acts of courage are countless), but by challenging and defeating his father, the old Patriarch, in single combat. Courageous acts that advance the empire are grounds for a brave Kzinti to earn a new hereditary name to pass on to his decedents. A full name also means that the Kzinti is given a better education, land, a harem, and the right to breed.

A Kzinti that has not earned a hereditary name is called by his profession, such as Speaker-to-Animals or Slaver-Student; these Kzinti often have tattoos on their ears displaying proficiency. Kzinti with partial names like Chuft-Captain represent intermediate recognition of noble birth, substantial service, or conspicuous gallantry. Addressing a Kzinti by his previous job-bearing title is a grievous insult.

The Patriarchy calls the last war with Earth the "Fourth Truce with Man." The Patriarchy does not understand why they have not been destroyed or enslaved by their former enemies, and is unwilling to accept that the Kzinti are, in many ways, respected for their bravery and courage.

Like many of Earth's governmental bodies, the Patriarchy keeps a great deal of information from its citizens, such as the secret to the Quantum II hyperdrive and the location of the Ringworld. Kzinti diplomats are often provided with these secrets, and many know more of mankind's relation to the Pak than most humans.

KDAPTISM

During the Man-Kzin wars, a strange religious faction appeared within the Kzinti ranks, worshipping the ideal of *Kdapt*. Kdaptism preached that the Creator made humans and *not* Kzinti, in his own image. Though this religion was most often the venue of low-born families, there were a few Kzinti in the greater nobility who also subscribed to Kdaptism.

When Kdaptist disciples prayed, they wore masks of human skin in the hopes of confusing the Creator long enough for the Kzinti to win the war. Human psychologists suggest that hundreds of years of steady losses of their greatest warriors tore at the social and psychological infrastructure of the Kzinti race, who believed their destiny to be no less than domination of the universe. The disbelief created by the losses in turn created Kdaptism.

When asked for their opinion about this theory, Kzinti mutter something untranslatable in the Hero's Tongue.

THE HERO'S TONGUE

The Hero's Tongue is the native Kzinti language, which to humans sounds like a series of rapid spittings and growlings; intonation and form are very important in conveying meaning.

The Hero's Script is fluid and nonlinear, taking the form of simple geometric patterns of dots and commas. Kzinti books are popular among human art collectors.

A KZINTI WARRIOR STANDS READY TO DIE

Major Races of Known Space

The Guide to Larry Niven's Ringworld

KZINTI UPBRINGING

The quality of a Kzinti's upbringing depends on nobility of birth, but training in the martial arts is common to every Kzinti male. The three martial levels are natural, primitive, and advanced. There are eight schools of the natural martial arts and each teaches a different technique, but in the true traditions of feudalism and aristocracy, the techniques of the more noble schools are better. This is one of the reasons that untitled or lower echelon nobility have little chance of defeating a higher ranking noble in combat.

Training in primitive weapon use is more a matter of tradition than practicality, as most Kzinti prefer to rely either on their natural martial arts training or a gun than the bone of an animal. However, the weapons held in the Patriarchy's war museum (the name of which cannot be translated out of the Hero's Tongue) frighten most humans to behold. The entrance hall is lined with hundreds of *sthondat*, primitive clubs made from the bones of the huge Kzin predators of the same name, much larger than the body of the average human. There are also two-handed axes which could easily fell a mature redwood and a collection of ancient *wtsai* blades, a polished black war knife cast in the shape of a Kzinti claw.

Advanced weapon use is seen by Kzinti as a duty, something that improves their ability to attack in the name of the Patriarchy. There are hundreds of variations of weapons to suit Kzinti needs, most of which out-size and outdistance human equivalents. Projectile weapons called heavy pistols by Kzinti must be lifted with two hands by most other races. Only very advanced weapons like the Slaver Disintegrator are kept relatively compact.

Fathers take an active interest in training their sons, taking them to the Kzin hunting parks that are stocked with predators and meat-animals. The kittens get the chance to hone their hunting skills and improve their reflexes. Kzinti enjoy hunting for their food and prefer to use their own teeth and claws to relying on weapons.

KZINTI HONOR

More than half of Kzinti kittens die in duels and hunting accidents. Overpopulation has never been a problem on Kzin; when there are too many Kzinti, the chance of accidental insult rises exponentially, meaning more duels and more deaths.

Points of honor are unaffected by time or distance. An insulted Kzinti remains insulted until he has either carried out his

A FATHER SHOWS HIS SON THE WAYS OF HUNTING

vengeance, died, or apologized, usually in that order. Kzinti carry out all threats and seldom bluff. They do not lie for politeness, and unintended insults are often mistaken for intended slights, requiring combat. Hazard pay for expeditions is considered an insult, as a Kzinti should not notice the danger.

Kzinti never sell their honor for profit and consider such an act unworthy of sentients. Their code stops them from verifying statements (even of prisoners) using a telepath, drugs, or other method as long as the captive does not lie.

In rare cases, a dishonored Kzinti may suffer the loss of one or both ears, claws, or even be forced to take a Kzinti version of boosterspice, which would erase all hard-won battle scars, the symbols of a Kzinti's courage and honor. A Kzinti may be killed or forced to duel with a member of the Patriarchy in even rarer events of treason, treachery, or heresy.

KZINTI FEMALES

Female Kzinti are non-sentient. They cannot manage their lives without male supervision, and do very little except, eat, sleep, and breed. Ancient Kzinti females were just as intelligent as the males, but they proved too bothersome to the patriarchal and stronger males. The females were slowly bred to lose their aggression and intelligence, a devolution taking millennia.

Each Kzinti family consists of a father and his male decedents. The females are treated as property or favorite pets. Favored females are protected because of the strong sons they bear and not out of personal devotion. Each noble keeps a harem large enough to fit his status and ability to protect. Most of the females are kept pregnant to maximize the number of heirs.

Humans who have regular contact with Kzinti diplomats (the most "liberal" of Kzinti) find their envy of intelligent females amusing.

KZIN TELEPATHS

Kzinti telepaths are forced addicts of a drug extracted from the *sthondat* lymph. Only one out of every thousand Kzinti telepaths retain their sanity, but become shivering neurotics. The effects of the drug are a major ordeal to even the most accomplished Kzinti telepaths; none will take a telepathy-inducing dose

A KZINTI TELEPATH STANDS READY TO COMPAIN

Major Races of Known Space — The Guide to Larry Niven's Ringworld

unless ordered. One dose of the drug lasts for eight hours, and the telepath must sleep for at least twenty hours afterward or suffer severe health problems.

Under the drug, the telepath lapses into a relaxed hypnotic state and can probe the minds of targets up to 2500 kilometers away. The ordeal is disgusting, painful, and exhausting for both the telepath and the target. Any person caught in the mental grip of a Kzinti telepath stiffens convulsively and experiences rolling waves of pain in the forehead and neck. The target may lose consciousness. Kzin telepaths can read the minds of any intelligent species except Bandersnatchi. Fortunately, they cannot induce a Slaver-like compulsion.

Kzinti telepaths are easily identified by their unkempt appearance, matted fur, and bouts of shivering. They sleep for most of their leisure hours. Their bedraggled, distraught appearance is shameful for a Kzinti.

Since the end of the last Man-Kzin war, Kzin telepaths are only encountered in espionage operations, piracy, and other illegal operations.

KZINTI IN KNOWN SPACE

Mankind's most dangerous enemy often finds himself the object of embarrassing attention while traveling in the company of humans. Kzinti often have trouble reconciling their peaceful trade with the aliens they once attempted attempted to conquer.

Kzinti are excellent mathematicians, and their race excels in the physical sciences. The Kzinti were the first to create the gravity polarizer, which allows crews to withstand high gravity accelerations. In addition, Kzinti medical supplies are superior to human supplies and are popular black market items.

IMPERIAL CONQUEROR CLASS DREADNOUGHT

The ARM maintains and guards the only Kzinti dreadnought to be captured intact during combat. The Imperial Conqueror class dreadnought mounts enough firepower to destroy the combined military strength of 20th century Earth. The ship is an ominous crimson sphere, 200 meters in diameter with ugly traces of black and silver. The captain's name is inscribed in a twenty meter circle of green commas and dots; the white bridge dome is set atop the sphere. The fifteen meter diameter blisters spaced around the equator of the ship are actually Scream-of-Vengeance interceptors.

The ship's armaments include fusion bombs, strike missiles, antimissile systems, laser cannons, disrupters, and induction projectors. Two latitudinal belts of hexagonal ports alternate with crystal-blue laser domes. There was enough power to cruise at .8 c and maintain maneuverability.

The nominal complement for the Imperial Conqueror was 512 of Kzin's fiercest warriors. The ARM will not reveal how the ship was captured.

PHYSIQUE

At a distance, Kzinti might resemble huge orange housecats, but nobody has ever mentioned this and lived. A male Kzinti can easily reach eight feet tall and weigh in excess of 200 kilograms. Their bodies are covered in a rich coat of orange-red fur that varies in coloration; yellow or white stripes, or black markings around the eyes are common. The members of the nobility often have their own unique colorations found only among their own named class. Kzinti tails are long, hairless, and ratlike.

Kzinti eyes are remarkably human, and they have round pupils instead of slitted pupils, like a terrestrial cat. Their ears are hairless and multi-pointed, held flat against their heads while they are calm or fanning out like parasols when angry or listening intently for the sound of prey.

Paws like black leather gloves provide sheaths for long, retractile claws which are sharpened and polished. Kzinti mouths are full of needle-like teeth for tearing raw flesh. Kzinti are famous for their grin. A Kzin grins when angry or challenging someone (or something), readying their teeth by exposing them in a deadly smile.

ALIEN RACES OF KNOWN SPACE

77	**BANDERSNATCHI**
81	**DOLPHINS**
85	**GROGS**
89	**KDATLYNO**
93	**OUTSIDERS**
97	**TRINOC**

BANDERSNATCHI

The strange Bandersnatchi are the only sentient species to survive the collapse of the Slaver empire. The Bandersnatchi were bio-engineered by the Tnuctipun race as meat animals for the Thrint (every part made delicious to the Slavers). It did not take long for the Bandersnatchi to become integrated into every part of Slaver society.

What the Thrint did not realize was that the Bandersnatchi were a trap set by the Tnuctipun. The Bandersnatchi were secretly given intelligence, immunity to the telepathic domination used by the Slavers, and high resistance to mutation that might occur on one of the Thrint dominated worlds to ensure the genetic stability of the first two critical traits. Information gathering for the Tnuctipun was the Bandersnatchi directive so that the slave races might find a way to overcome their captors.

THE TNUCTIPUN COUP

It took several centuries for the Tnuctipun to gather enough information from their espionage network to stage a rebellion. The Bandersnatchi destroyed many Slaver planet enclaves within the first year. The Thrint were remarkably slow to realize that their empire was on the verge of collapse and they underestimated the strengths of their slaves. After several more years and the increasing losses of critical planets and planetary systems, the Slavers sacrificed their entire enclave to save themselves by commanding their slaves to destroy themselves. Thanks to the foresight of the Tnuctipun bio-engineers, only the Bandersnatchi were immune to the effects of the Thrint thought amplifiers which forced the mass suicide of all other races. Ironically, the Slaver regime collapsed and the Thrint race died because of their dependency on their subject races to provide food and maintain the machines of empire.

The Slaver race died two billion years before the discovery of the Ringworld. The Bandersnatchi immunity to random genetic mutation allowed the race to survive on many worlds throughout Known Space and the areas once controlled by the Thrint, especially previous Slaver food planets where the Bandersnatchi were most prevalent. The Bandersnatchi were isolated on Jinx for hundreds of years, living in the heat and heavy fog, feeding off the gray food yeast on the ocean shorelines. Their isolation was more than just separation from other races. Their complete domination of the lowlands prevented other forms of life from evolving.

Alien Races of Known Space — *The Guide to Larry Niven's Ringworld*

A Bandersnatch's life consisted of little more than eating and the company of others of its race. They gradually lost detailed knowledge of their origins, even the reason for which they were created and how they arrived on Jinx. The stories they told each other were constantly told, altered, and retold.

FIRST CONTACT WITH THE BANDERSNATCHI

The Bandersnatchi were first discovered on Jinx by human colonists in 2097 A.D., who took the creatures to be non-intelligent. After a few skirmishes the humans changed their view. The first attempts at communication often wound up with the colonist accidentally crushed by the bulk of a Bandersnatch and the start of another skirmish. Fortunately, the Bandersnatchi remembered something of the scientific language used by the Tnuctipun. An information exchange was established followed by the founding of the famous Institute of Knowledge. The Bandersnatchi were eventually able to give the Institute fascinating data, both on the history of the long dead Slaver empire, as well as scientific advances of the Tnuctipun.

Some Jinxian professors at the Institute of Knowledge have degrees in Bandersnatchi communication. The most common method of communication involves the use of psionic-contact equipment, similar to that used to speak with dolphins and other Cetaceans. The Bandersnatchi communication equipment is much more complex than that used for dolphins, using more power and greater skill. The results can still be confusing, and, many times, frustrating.

Strangely, human scientists do not consider the Bandersnatchi to be possible dangers despite the race's artificial origins. There has been speculation by some of the scientists at the Institute of Knowledge that the Tnuctipun may have created a device similar to the Slaver thought amplifier to control the Bandersnatchi. They argue that the number of thematically similar inventions found throughout Known Space (such as the addictive power of the tasp and vampire essence) would suggest such an item must exist. The Bandersnatchi claim to know nothing about such a device, either biological or technological.

BANDERSNATCHI APPEARANCE

A Bandersnatch weighs somewhere between 30 and 60 tons

and resembles a monstrous white slug. A long neck begins in a sloping cone somewhere near the creature's "shoulders," ending in a rounded tip adorned by nothing more than tufts of black hair on the sides. A moving Bandersnatch looks similar to a whale swimming through sand; its long neck sways left and right without apparent purpose. Like a slug, the Bandersnatch uses a belly-foot to drag itself along the ground. It scoops yeast and edible swamp-scum through a toothless mouth located in front of the belly-foot.

The Institute scientists discovered something of Bandersnatchi origins by studying the creatures' physiology. The most interesting Bandersnatchi feature is the lack of cell walls and anything having to do with cellular reproduction; they are made of nothing but specialized protoplasm. Healing is more a process of organic compound redistribution than of cell regrowth. Bandersnatchi nerves appear to act like human nerves, but without nuclei and "standardized" functions, such as axons. All these strange bundles of protoplasms lead to the brains, whose topography baffles the holographic rendering abilities of the most advanced Known Space computers. The brain itself is located in the hard shell of the Bandersnatchi neck.

A Bandersnatch has five huge hearts, each weighing about five kilograms. The creature's circulatory systems is navigated by a series of veins and canals, the veins leading from the hearts, and the canals leading back. Bandersnatchi blood is pale white and in many ways could be considered a single protoplasmic entity. It is the blood of the Bandersnatch that makes its deathly white skin change to an icy blue color under sunlight, such as found on certain parts of Jinx. It is not known whether this is a defense mechanism of unknown purpose or a natural reaction. Bandersnatchi skin does not contain anything equivalent to melanin, the substance that darkens a human skin under ultraviolet radiation.

The hairs at the end of the Bandersnatch "head" are actually its main sense organs. The hairs sway constantly, registering change in potentials, such as air temperature, light intensity, and scent. Bandersnatchi communicate by interlocking their sense organs and registering their rustlings. They also communicate through ground vibration and "reading" the tracks their huge bodies make in the ground. The tracks are the race's only written history, and it does not take long for the furrows to become confused by other tracks and the erosion caused by weather.

A CURIOUS BANDERSNATCH EYES THE CAMERA

DOLPHINS

A great majority of human history denoted dolphins as nothing more than creatures of the sea, like any other fish. It was not until the 20th century, thanks to the pioneering work of Lilly, and the later Institute for Delphinological Studies, that humanity realized it had created an unnecessary segregation with one of the most intelligent species on Earth.

The Cetacean Rights Act of 2017 banned all whaling and granted sentient species the equivalence of full human protection. As the years went by, dolphins entered the United Nations and created treaties with the world. Coastal embassies were established in Newfoundland, St. Thomas, Baja, Hawaii, Opononi, Sydney, Sri Lanka, Brazil, Japan, and in the Mediterranean. The dolphins also began grievance suits for past damages in international courts of law.

No settlements were ever reached.

CONTACT

Humans can experience the exotic and rich world-view of dolphins using two techniques that require telepathic aptitude. The first involves the use of a helmet developed in the 21st century which allows a partial (and mutual) transfer of memory and images. These crystal-iron psionic devices are said to have given the dolphins their first taste of the stars, while humans were awarded with the dolphins' view of the world ecology.

Fully psionic humans are capable of contacting dolphins directly, enjoying what is described as a, "truly transcendental experience." Words used to illustrate the experience are "musical," "joyous," "euphoric," and "visionary."

The acoustic songs of the dolphin philosopher-historians have given humans insight into areas that normal metaphysics is incapable of addressing. The processes of nature, events and their causes, and logical proofs coalesce within these dreamsongs.

Few humans can give back to the dolphins what knowledge of mysteries they have received. Dolphins say the best thing humans have to offer back is love.

DOLPHINS AND SOCIETY

Dolphins are very social and display characteristics similar to humans. Most of their communication amongst themselves deals with relationships, both personal and social. Their codes of ethics and conducts of behavior are as diverse as humanity's, but few dolphins are prone to violence.

It took a great deal of time for humans to realize that dolphins are not benign, super-visionary pacifists. Some dolphins eagerly embraced a number of human vices. One band of notorious dolphins hijacked a starship.

Dolphins are always amazed, and sometimes appalled, by the human fascination with control of territory and accumulation of wealth. This led to in-depth study by the dolphins of humanity. Many close relationships developed between dolphins and humans, some of them physical. The humans describe the dolphins as being gentle, compassionate, and sensual.

Dolphins are offered the same education as any human on the Earth, including study of religion, government, meta-linguistics, and literature.

HANDS BY GARVEY LIMITED

Thumbists were a faction of humanity who believed that sentient creatures who lacked thumbs were handicapped. The entrepreneurs at Garvey Limited made fortunes selling psionic/prosthetic Hands to dolphins and to delphinetarian organizations (mostly sympathetic thumbists) who wanted to help the dolphins integrate more easily into society.

Dolphins changed the face of hundreds of industries, especially sea farming and undersea paleontology. Navigation and salvage was revolutionized when satellite links were provided to the dolphins. The suits that permit dolphins to walk on land and in space are called "walker suits."

As a sidenote, most dolphins feel that tactile use of the environment dubious and crude entertainment.

PHYSIOLOGY AND PERCEPTIONS

Tursiops truncata, commonly called the bottle-nosed dolphin, is the best known of the dolphin species. Their coloration ranges from dark brown to black, and sometimes albino. Tursiops are typically two or three meters long and can weigh as much as two hundred kilograms.

Dolphin vision is sharp, but they have little sense of smell. They sometimes track their prey through their sense of taste, following trails of "flavor" through the sea. They acquire their fresh water from their prey.

Dolphins "see" and communicate with sound through three sonic/ultrasonic transmitters, two in the blowhole and one in the larynx. This gives the dolphin 360° solid-angle or tight-beam sonar views. This provides excellent three-dimensional pictures and allows dolphins to communicate with each other very quickly, even over distances of several kilometers.

DELPHINESE

Delphinese is the language used by dolphins, sounding like a series of chirps, clicks, burps, creaks, hoots, and other sounds. Each dolphin has a unique style of speaking and tone.

Humans are basically incapable of speaking delphinese, but some dolphins have been able to emulate human speech, sounding like a screeching child. Humans usually give dolphins names they can pronounce and gesture a great deal to get their points across when no translation equipment is available.

DR. MENA SWANSON

One of the few humans who can speak a fraction of delphinese, Dr. Swanson is a known advocate of dolphin rights in Known Space and actively campaigns in the United Nations. She is favored amongst the dolphin population, who write many songs and poems in her name, which they shorten in their dedications to, "M."

A DOLPHIN PREPARES TO LITIGATE FROM ITS UNDERWATER HOME

GROGS

Grogs are a bizarre race native to Down who possess strong powers of telepathy. The Kzinti who controlled Down (before it was annexed in the first Man-Kzin war) never suspected that the Grogs were intelligent. The Grogs themselves never let their intelligence or their telepathic ability be known to the invaders. After the war, many human colonists considered the Grogs to be nothing more than curiosities.

THE GROG LIFE CYCLE

The Grogs have a two stage life cycle. In the first stage, they are small and fierce quadrupeds with the intelligence of a dog. The female appears to be a poor attempt to construct a bulldog. The males are about the size of Chihuahuas. Both are covered in long, reddish hair for camouflage in the desert light cast by the planet's red dwarf sun.

Young Grogs are as temperamental as their appearance would suggest. They yip and snarl, bite, growl, and otherwise carry on, growing quickly and finding a mate. The female finds a rock to sit on and settles down, continually growing and having children. The males never grow beyond their little-dog size, and are kept as pets by the females.

GROG TELEPATHY

The Grog spinal chord and nerves are degenerate. However, the brain of the Grog is bigger than a basketball, weighing about twenty-five kilograms. This puzzled scientists of the Laboratory for Xenobiological Research on Down after colonization, who took six or seven Grogs to the facility for research. The captive Grogs were afraid to show their intelligence to the humans in much the same way they were afraid with the Kzinti. They finally contacted humanity through a representative of Garvey Limited, the company that manufactures Dolphin's Hands prosthetics.

The Grogs do not need to move from their rock because they can control any animal within a few hundred meters, calling their food when hungry. They can use the senses of whatever animal is under their control (including humans), which explained the Grogs' minimal sensory organs.

Grogs can lodge irresistible commands in the minds of sentient beings. No knowledge of language is required for this to work. The only known defense is the extremely rare Slaver mind-shield power present in a few telepathic humans. A Grog suggestion has unusual clarity and is held with the utmost conviction, two traits not commonly associated with the sea of doubt and probability common in human thought.

Grogs claim that their power's maximum range is half way around Down, with all of them linked in concert. The Grogs are unable to control Bandersnatchi, who are immune to all forms of telepathic domination.

COMMUNICATING WITH GROGS

The Grogs have emigrated to a number of human worlds as tourists and residents. They require special protection from ultraviolet radiation and travel in enclosed MAGLEV couches large enough to hold the Grog and her rock.

Communicating with Grogs is typically performed through computers and printers since most humans do not like direct telepathic contact. Grog often act as translators, security guards, and veracity-verification officers in important legal proceedings.

GROGOPHOBIA

Grogs are friendly and cooperative. They have made no known attempts at manipulation and have made substantial contributions to Known Space.

However, the Grogs inspire paranoia in many races, especially humans. Factions of governments call for the extermination of the race on the basis that they are too powerful to let loose in the galaxy, basing their idea on the legacy of the Slaver empire from billions of years ago. To allay Grogophobia, a huge fusion ramship has been placed in orbit around Down's sun. If the engines were started, the electromagnetic ramscoop field would cause the sun to flare in the ultraviolet range, destroying all unprotected forms of life on the planet (and the Grogs are especially susceptible to UV radiation).

True Grogophobists are not assuaged by this gesture. Their paranoia builds on itself, and they say that the Grogs are able to convince the crew of the ramship that all systems are operational, even when they're not. Those people suffering from acute Grogophobia believe that the Grogs have already taken over Known Space but nobody could know it.

ADULT GROG PHYSIOLOGY

A Grog is a comical one and a half meter high hairy cone firmly attached to a rock a little over a meter in diameter. Grogs are incapable of moving, and their limbs are useless. Long, straight, reddish hair falls over the top of the rock like a skirt; the top is rounded and bald. There are no eyes or ears. Two small paws poke through the hair, naked and pink, while two vestigial hands with curved fingers appear a meter above the paws.

The meter long lipless mouth is placed above the forepaws; when closed, the edges curl up into a gentle grin. The Grog's prehensile tongue is as fast as any reptile's and has enough dexterity to operate tools and computers.

SLUG-A-GROG

Despite the propensity for many humans to fear Grogs and their immense psionic powers, there are a number of people who actually enjoy the company of Grogs. The Grogs get along very well with humans, but are sometimes prone to be the brunt of a few practical jokes, the most popular of which is known as "slug-a-Grog."

Slug-a-Grog is usually played by three or four people, usually interns from the Laboratory for Xenobiological Research on Down, after long tests or research runs. The most common way to play is to quietly erect a tent near a sleeping Grog (whose physical senses are so minimal that loud noises rarely wake them anyway) and drink heavily, usually bourbon, whiskey, or whatever can be synthesized in the labs.

When the Grog awakes, it's usually curious as to what's in the tent and makes telepathic contact with the interns, who are either dead drunk or nursing terrible hangovers. The result seems to knock the smug grin off any Grog.

Most scientists feel this game to be extremely juvenile and have sought ways to have the interns punished. However, interns are the only ones who seem to have any free time to distill and are the only suppliers of liquor to otherwise "dry" facilities, so they are usually left alone.

A GROG TELEPATHICALLY INSTRUCTS THE ILLUSTRATOR...

The Guide to Larry Niven's Ringworld — *Alien Races of Known Space*

KDATLYNO

The Kdatlyno are a race of nightmarish giants whose homeworld is twenty-seven light years from Earth. They are completely blind, using sonics to "see" their surroundings. Their philosophy states that every great revelation carries with it a greater challenge, and ideas unsculpted by actions are unaesthetic.

When they achieved the science to leave Kdat, they colonized other worlds, traveling in enormous ships powered by nuclear-ion engines. They used the 21 centimeter interstellar hydrogen band to contact other life forms in the galaxy.

THE KDAT-KZIN WAR

The Kzinti were always waiting for other species to use the 21 centimeter band. When the Kdatlyno sent their initial messages, the Kzinti began their plans to conquer Kdat, enslave the inhabitants, and take the resources. The first Kzinti ships arrived at the outer edges of the Kdat system and destroyed the few Kdatlyno vessels on their way out. The Kzinti ships were ready for war and had the advantage of surprise, while the Kdatlyno ships were large, slow, and not well-armed.

At first notice of the invading ships, the Kdatlyno recalled all available vessels into the Kdat system to form picket defense lines against the Kzinti. Nuclear missiles were converted into mines because the Kzinti antimissile defenses were usually too accurate for the Kdatlyno missiles to score any hits. The war was long and savage, but the Kzinti had no doubt they would be victorious.

Strength and determination won the Kdatlyno the respect of their captors. A few escaped to the hidden caverns and chambers of their ancestors before the Kzinti managed to enslave all the Kdatlyno. The Kzinti used the Kdatlyno to mine their own world and build Kzinti ships. The second Man-Kzin war released the Kdatlyno from their captors centuries later.

RECOVERING AFTER THE PATRIARCHY

The Kdatlyno culture had nearly been obliterated. The remains were preserved by the few who had managed to escape slavery in the caverns beneath the ground. Their planets had been ransacked and Earth was not as willing to give them aid as it had been to liberate them; Earth and her colonies had no time to help the seemingly ungrateful and antisocial aliens.

Alien Races of Known Space · The Guide to Larry Niven's Ringworld

The Kdatlyno negotiated major industrial contracts, finding their immense strength and unique visual abilities gave them a wide variety of employment opportunities. The race finally entered fully into the Known Space economy after 400 years.

TOUCH SCULPTURE

The Kdatlyno aesthetic sense is expressed in a unique and intriguing art form called *touch sculpture*. Touch sculptures are meant only to be sensed with the Kdatlyno sonic sight, a sculpture's oscillations and reflections carrying strong emotional themes. Humans see pure touch sculpture as unfathomably bland. They are unable to notice that the soul of the art is also expressed in its internal forms created by the blend of its substances, contoured boundary-layers, and inner resonant cavities.

An innovative school of touch-sculpture was started in the late 2500s by Hrodenu and Lloobee. They were the first to combine human representational conceits with Kdatlyno ideas. Their works are prized all over Known Space. Touch sculpture often captures the imagination of amateur artists, but the extreme skill and remarkable patience required to create a touch sculpture often drives most students away.

KDATLYNO VENGEANCE

The formidable size and presence of the Kdatlyno makes most humans feel ill at ease. Humans feel the race to be unpredictable and easily aggravated by trivial matters. The main reason for this behavior is that humans most often encounter Kdatlyno in confined spaces, such as spacecraft, where the race feels the most uncomfortable and is likely to be difficult.

The Kdatlyno sense of honor is as strongly developed as the Kzinti. Any deliberate insult or injury is grounds for retaliation, either immediately or whenever is appropriate. If the matter is truly grave, then death may be the only solution. Kdatlyno will occasionally avenge friends or relatives, but personal affronts elicit the most intricate and devastating plots.

Humans do not understand Kdatlyno behavior and simply label the race as difficult and antisocial. Humans unfairly characterize Kdatlyno culture as a series of unending feuds and vengeances. Some social experts theorize that the Kdatlyno as a race are plotting their greatest revenge against the Kzinti.

KDATLYNO PHYSIOLOGY

The average Kdatlyno reaches an average height of three to four meters and often weighs more than a ton. They have thick, dark brown skin, like lizard hide, which is thick enough to stop a knife. Each hand has four retractable claws at the knuckle, and their armored knee and elbow joints have curved horns and silver-tipped spikes. Kdatlyno are surprisingly swift and agile, even in water.

The Kdatlyno are blind to visible light, but possess a sophisticated sonic radar sense. A goggle-shaped organ covered by a taut membrane acts as a sonic transducer. Each Kdatlyno sends out a unique ultrasonic signal that give the alien a detailed picture, including distance, density, and textures. At close range, the Kdatlyno can "see" into normal materials and detect underlying details, such as the pipes behind a spaceship's inner hull.

Female Kdatlyno (called Kdatlyn) mate with five to fifteen compatible males over a period of twenty to sixty days. Many fathers' contributions are lost before fertilization begins. Multiple births are the rule.

NIGEL PEREZ, ESQ.

Nigel is one of the best-known touch-sculptors in the avant-garde circles of Known Space. His most famous piece, *Sonic Boom*, is considered by many Kdatlyno to be a superior work of art.

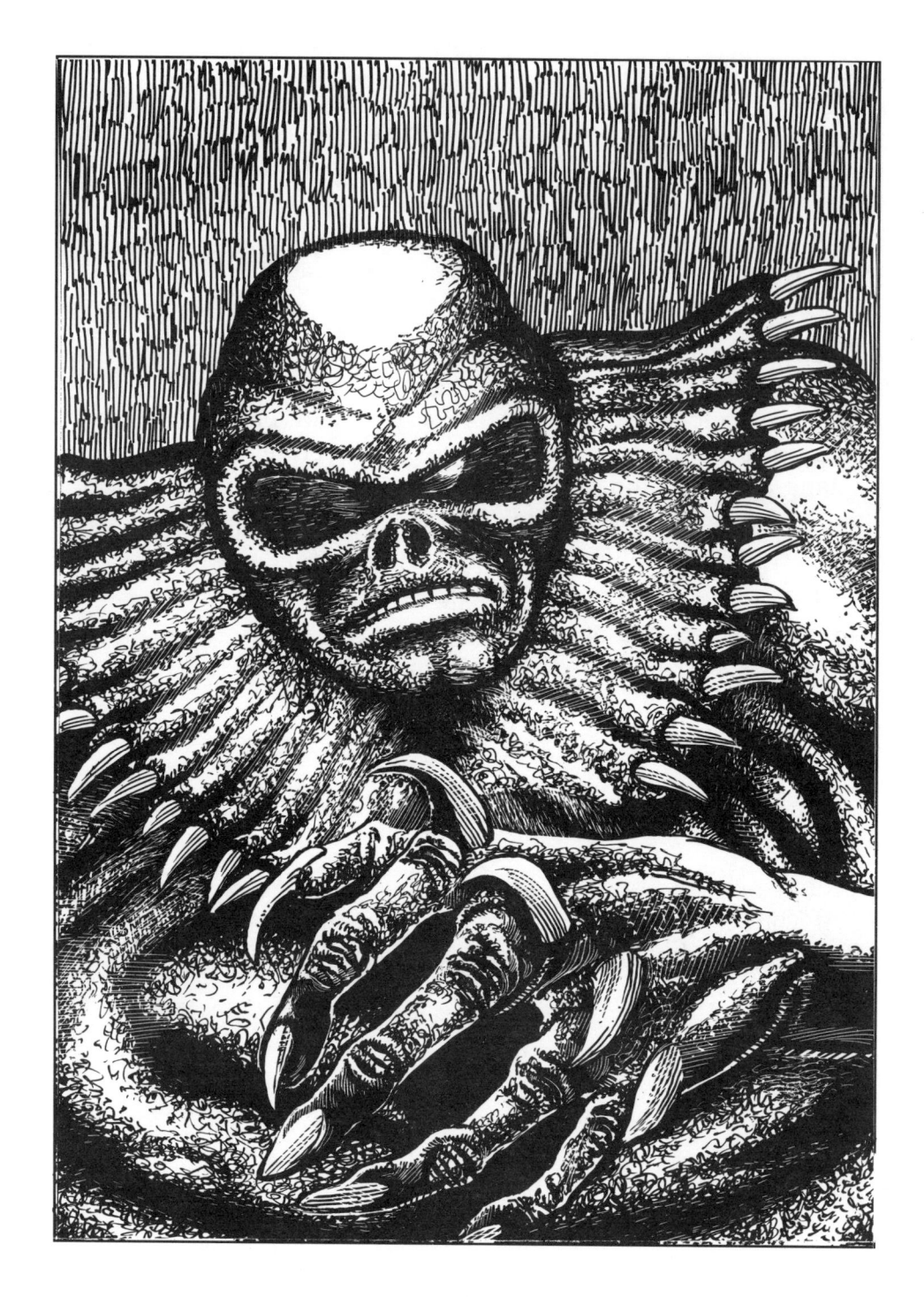

A KDATLYNO ON THE VERGE OF A CLAUSTROPHOBIC OUTBURST

OUTSIDERS

The Outsiders are the most unearthly of the alien races encountered by humankind. Cold, fragile beings adapted to life in outer space, Outsiders are enigmatic, outwardly paradoxical, and never thoroughly grasped by humans.

OUTSIDER BUSINESS

The Outsiders spend most of their time searching the galaxy for starseeds or selling information. The Outsiders are known to honor any deal they initiate, and are equally known for their shrewdness and business acumen.

Outsiders with information to sell usually send out a broadband transmission before actually arriving in a system. The prices are clearly defined, though the information is typically mysterious. The Outsider standard cost for truly interesting information (such as why they follow starseeds) is one trillion Stars. The information Outsiders buy is usually equal to the cost of the information they sell, knowing that they will be able to quickly make back their loss by selling to many systems and races. Most often, the money for information bought by the Outsiders is applied either as credit for future transactions or credit reduction for previous transactions.

When a planetary system harbors a suitable world and potential customers, Outsiders may rent space, setting up trade centers, rest and recreation areas, and supply dumps. As an example, the Outsiders leased Nereid, the smaller moon of Neptune, as a base in the solar system. They continue to beam communiques long after they have established friendly contact with the system and have never been known to leave a sales region once established.

Outsiders never argue over a price, and do not employ blackmail or other practices like the Puppeteers as part of business. Information about dangerous events costs a little more than normal.

There is no center for Outsider operations. Their ships rarely have information about previous Outsider contacts. When contacting alien species, Outsiders always give their ships numbers, never names. This ensures the most neutral setting for negotiations.

OUTSIDER SHIPS

The majority of an Outsider interstellar ship is made up of empty space where the Outsiders can bask in sunlight, their primary source of nourishment. The population of an Outsider ship is equal to most small cities, but the ship is made much larger to accommodate the basking areas.

Most Outsider ships have a large cylinder located near the center of its mass, housing a reactionless, intertialess drive capable of thousand gee accelerations. Other Outsider vessels use photon sails, much like those of the early Earth ramships. The Outsiders always travel in normal Einsteinian space and think that hyperdrive is vulgar.

The rest of the Outsider ship is made of winding ribbons the width of a human city sidewalk that sweep in and among themselves, creating tangled archways of light and darkness. In addition, all Outsider craft have artificial light sources to simulate suns when the ship is too far to receive sufficient emissions. The light is mounted on a pole four kilometers long, appearing as small and yellow as Earth's sun seen from Neptune. The reason for this design is that the Outsiders gain their nutrients through thermoelectricity; the difference in temperature from the lit zone to the shadow zone creates currents in their bodies, recharging their biochemical batteries.

Most species find Outsider ships disquieting.

OUTSIDERS AND STARSEEDS

The Outsiders are an enigma to Known Space, but one of their most intriguing mysteries is their interest in starseeds.

Starseeds are huge, mindless creatures which lived in the galactic core before it exploded. They feed on hydrogen-rich interstellar gas, riding the photon winds to deposit their fertilized eggs in the outer tips of the galaxy's spiral arms. Experts believe that some of the eggs are actually launched at the Clouds of Magellan or Andromeda.

When the eggs hatch, the newly birthed starseed chick makes its way back toward the galactic core, about 50,000 light years at an average speed of .8 c. The chick stays folded in a compact ovoid two or three kilometers wide for the majority of the trip, executing course change without apparent reason. The course change is performed with a photon sail, a silvery parachute attached to the chick's body through four shrouds. The mirrorlike sail is no more than a millimeter thick but is thousands of kilometers wide. A cross-shaped thickening in the sail is the body of the starseed, and a knob hanging from the shrouds are the muscles that control the sail and another egg.

Outsiders are willing to sell secret of their relation to starseeds for the usual price.

OUTSIDER PHYSIOLOGY
Outsiders resemble black cat-o'-nine-tail whips with large handles. Their brains and sense organs are located in the handles, as well as the biochemical batteries which give them life. Their metabolism is based on liquid helium, an excellent medium for generating thermoelectricity. Strangely, there are a number of alien species based on helium II except they are all planet-bound and nonsentient.

The whips are a dextrous cluster of root-tentacles which contain weak gas jets to propel an Outsider through the void of space. The whip cluster is also used to draw nutrients and important trace elements suspended in liquid helium.

From the use of these weak gas jets and other evidence, it is inferred that the Outsiders' ancestors were plantlike creatures native to the small moon of a gas giant. Since the Outsiders are incapable of withstanding even light gravity, it is further guessed that the moon itself may have been a series of asteroids or perhaps a proto-moon, composed of little more than gas, a few rocks, and enough biological building blocks to create life.

The Outsiders communicate through unknown means. When they speak to other races, they are able to use, through equipment, whatever communications techniques are natural to the customer.

There are no Outsiders on Ringworld.

LAUREN MARIE NYSTUL
Lauren is an extremely wealthy woman who received her money from an inheritance of a simulation game company. She is also an ARM agent who has had many dealings with the Outsiders, some without her superior's knowledge.

*AN OUTSIDER BASKS
IN THE HALF-LIGHT OF ITS SHIP*

TRINOCS

The first publicized meeting between the Trinocs and humanity occurred in a system about forty light years from Earth by none other than Louis Wu. Louis was scouring the system with deep radar, searching for Slaver artifacts when he had a confrontation with a Trinoc scout craft. They had both discovered a mysterious ball of neutronium orbiting one of the planets.

The strange cone-shaped craft of the trinocs used a sophisticated intertialess drive capable of tremendous accelerations. Contact with its crew of six was established through conventional communication lasers and auto-pilot translators.

The Kzinti had known of the Trinocs for many years. The race was kept a secret from Earth, but there were many rumors during the Man-Kzin wars of a methane-breathing race beyond the fringes of Known Space that continually defied the Patriarchy.

The area controlled by the Trinocs is larger than Human Space, lying toward the constellations of Hercules, Ophiuchus, and northern Scorpius. Treaties state that officially, Trinoc space begins seven light years past Margrave.

The Puppeteers say they have traded with the Trinocs for many centuries through robotic probes. Nobody has been able to confirm this claim.

TRINOCS AND ALIENS

The Trinoc civilization has not expanded into space as quickly as humanity. This is attributed to the Trinoc ability to travel in a state of hibernation during sub-light travel. They only make limited use of Puppeteer hyperdrive ships, and have less of a need to hurry to their destinations, as humans often did before the discovery of boosterspice and the purchase of the Quantum I hyperdrive shunt.

Trinocs are not xenophobic or manipulative, and only attack if they perceive a sufficient threat to their activities. To this end, there are many treaties with human governments that prohibit the terraforming of Trinoc-habitable worlds. There is also a small Trinoc base on Titan.

Trinoc are not friendly toward other species. They are extremely cryptic and non-communicative, and most humans find them hostile or paranoid. The Trinoc are suspicious of others, and experts at hiding their intentions and motives. They say, "the process of living is a game of chance. Trying to avoid chance is insanity—but one must take only the risks required to win the game." The Trinocs Interworld name for what they call themselves is, "we-who-see-undeceived."

The Trinoc play games well. It is probably not a good idea to play poker with a Trinoc.

TRINOC PHYSIOLOGY

Few humans have visited Trinoc. It is a cold, low gravity world with an atmosphere inhospitable to any sentient Known Space species. The air is filled with a noxious orange-brown haze composed of methane, ammonia, water vapor, carbon dioxide, and nitrogen in a mixture of gases similar to primitive Earth. The reducing atmosphere also has large amounts of hydrogen cyanide, hydrogen sulfide, and formaldehyde. Titan would resemble Trinoc if it had been able to hold more hydrogen.

The origins of the Trinocs is a mystery. It is suspected that nucleotide synthesis may have occurred on the surface of clay-like substances containing flat-plate crystals of magnesium, aluminum, and silicon. Carbon compounds from cometary debris may have introduced organic catalysts. Self-replicating aggregates, similar to RNA, may have developed, giving the molecules both functional and information carrying properties. The double-helix of carbon based life was replaced by a great variety of molecular structures and three-dimensional foldings.

Trinoc physiology is not cellular, appearing to have a loosely organized metabolism. The metabolism is able to tolerate a great number of genetic errors during protoplasmic growth without encountering dangerous mutation.

Trinocs reproduce asexually, involving the exchange of several hundred milliliters of protoplasm amongst two or more Trinocs. This usually does nothing more than revitalize the Trinocs' metabolism, but occasionally the reproductive cycle triggers. Polyps appear on one or all the Trinocs within a few days, and are then placed in nutrient baths. The polyps who survive mature into infant Trinoc, who are given considerable attention by the parent.

APPEARANCE

Trinocs stand one and a half meters tall, a meter of which is skinny legs. The torso is barrel-shaped and covered by thick rolls of chrome-yellow skin from the head, hiding anatomical details. Two strong, spindly arms ending in three-clawed hands are located on either side of the torso.

A Trinoc's head appears to be made of triangles. The sense organs are located around its sharp-toothed, three lipped mouth. Each of the three round, blank eyes stares with a green pupil, giving the alien Trinocular vision.

A Trinoc can whip its head around to face backwards, then face back through a "universal socket" joint. This ability makes it difficult to sneak up on a Trinoc, though its origins are not understood since the Trinocs never had to worry about dangerous predators.

A TRINOC STANDS IN ITS POISONOUS ATMOSPHERE

THE LANDSCAPE OF RINGWORLD

103	SCRITH AND THE SUPERCONDUTOR GRID
105	ECOLOGY AND LIFE
108	THE GREAT OCEANS
113	METEOR DEFENSE SYSTEM
117	SHADOW SQUARES AND SHADOW SQUARE WIRE
119	RIM WALLS
122	SPACEPORT LANDING SYSTEM
125	RIM TRANSPORT SYSTEM

RINGWORLD
COMPOSITION AND FEATURES

SPILL MOUNTAINS AND RIM WALL SECTION

Legend:
- ▨ - TOP SOIL
- ▦ - BEDROCK
- ■ - SCRITH

Labels:
- RIMWALL
- SPILL MOUNTAINS
- FIST OF GOD MOUNTAINS
- OCEAN OR LAKE
- SPACEPORT LANDING SYSTEM
- RIMWALL
- ATTITUDE JET

NOTE: NOT TO SCALE

The Guide to Larry Niven's Ringworld — *The Landscape of Ringworld*

SCRITH AND THE SUPERCONDUCTOR GRID

Scrith is the hardest substance known to any race, millions of times denser than lead with properties unheard of in any material. The tensile strength of scrith is billions of times greater than terrestrial tungsten steel, much like General Products hulls or Slaver stasis fields.

The base material of Ringworld is scrith. Scrith is so indestructible that it withstands the hellish rotational velocity of Ringworld (1,232 kilometers per second). The floor of Ringworld is at least fifty to a hundred feet of solid scrith, and a foamed variant of scrith makes up another kilometer of depth.

In addition to its impossible strength, scrith is also nearly frictionless. On the surface of Ringworld, areas of exposed scrith appear to shimmer like dirty ice, grayish and nearly translucent. The soil and bedrock of Ringworld sit on top of the scrith superstructure. If someone were to be trapped in an area where there was nothing but bare scrith to walk on, that person would most likely die of starvation before reaching "dry" land.

The mass of Ringworld is similar to Jupiter, about 2×10^{30} grams, the majority of which is scrith. It is theorized that scrith was converted from the material of Jovian worlds through an unknown process.

SCRITH AND CZILTANG BRONES

Another fantastic property of scrith is its immutability. Scrith cannot be worked by any tool developed in Known Space. Neither Slaver nor Puppeteer disintegrators affect scrith; flashlight lasers are not reflected by scrith, and the target-point of the beam does not glow with heat. In fact, scrith absorbs forty percent of all neutrinos (which would not be affected by several light years of solid lead). Hyperwave transmissions are impossible through scrith, even if the scrith is limited to a few inches thickness, such as near the spill mountains.

The absorbing property of scrith will protect the inhabitants of Ringworld from the radiation shockwave caused by the galaxy core explosion. The wave will hit Known Space in 20,000 years and either mutate or kill all life forms except those who escape to Ringworld.

The City Builders discovered machines which rendered scrith permeable to solid matter, allowing people to "swim" through the tunnel, as if against a great wind. These machines were called *cziltang brones*, and many were used as fixed emplacements to allow access from one side of Ringworld to the other (since scrith cannot be worked, there is no way for portals or airlocks to be constructed to allow access).

Most of the cziltang brones were ruined during the superconductor plague and the City Builders have apparently lost the knowledge of their construction. Some of the devices failed during use, trapping crews inside the walls of scrith, killing them outright. Repairing the cziltang brones is extremely dangerous, since the beam of the machine can render biological membranes too permeable for normal "operation," killing the unfortunate victim.

SCRITH AND MAGLEV

Scrith can maintain an induced electromagnetic field, a feature of paramount importance to the inhabitants of Ringworld. Everything from simple dollies and platforms to aircraft and floating cities employ scrith repulsion systems (also called magnetic levitation, or MAGLEV), which are energy efficient and environmentally clean. Using scrith repulsion requires compensation for thrust in multiple directions if a craft flies near an angled surface, such as a mountain slope.

The only drawback to MAGLEV vehicles is their vulnerability to outside influence. Police fields were often employed by the City Builders to override the engines and controls of MAGLEV vehicles moving too quickly through the towers and spires of the floating cities. Microwave bursts also tend to disrupt the repulsion systems.

Many vehicles used superconductors in their drive units, but the superconductor plague destroyed the majority of these systems.

SUPERCONDUCTOR GRID

Much of Ringworld's operation depends on electromagnetic energy, especially for the meteor defense system. Electromagnetic energy runs through the scrith through huge hexagons of embedded superconductor cable. Twenty-three hexes stretch across the width of Ringworld, and about sixteen thousand extend along the length, making for approximately 350,000 hexes. The vertices from two out of three hexagons lead into and away from the spill mountains and along the rim through the third.

The only known nexus of the superconductor grid lies in the Map of Mars in the Oval Ocean. The power of the grid may be redirected and adjusted from the nexus control center for controlling the meteor defense system; any other uses are unknown.

The superconductor grid is not vulnerable to the superconductor plague which ravaged the artifacts of the civilizations on the surface of Ringworld.

ECOLOGY AND LIFE

The Ringworld Engineers built Ringworld to resemble terrestrial worlds, bonding bedrock to the scrith superstructure and putting soil on the surface. The ring spins at 1,232 kilometers per second to create artificial gravity through centrifugal force. The scrith was pre-structured to create mountains, seas, and coastlines. The rim walls keep the atmosphere from spilling out into space. The shadow squares create intervals of night and day. Moderate surface temperature is maintained by the shadow squares as well as by the superconductor grid embedded in the structural scrith; superconducting material maintains an even temperature and ensures that no part of the ring surface rises too high above 62° Fahrenheit.

Wind patterns were created to provide atmospheric circulation. Jet streams and countercurrents assist in the counter-erosion process, as do sculpted rivers and valleys. The rim walls and spill mountains are the main line of erosion defense.

FAILURE OF THE ACTIVE ECOLOGICAL DEFENSES

Climate control stations check local regulation of atmospheric moisture content, water table acidity, and other factors. Water condensation units are spaced around the perimeter of the superconductor grid's hexagons. Originally, these units prevented firestorms from occurring, but the superconductor plague disabled many of the units, creating disaster. The results of the storms have worn the landscape down to the scrith. In addition, the dredges that recycled flup from the bottom of the sea have also shut down, slowing or stopping the reclamation of valuable earth in many areas.

The superconductor plague is not the only cause of Ringworld's problems. The Ringworld Engineers could not anticipate every puncture in the scrith, such as the one that created Fist-of-God mountain. Eyestorms, shockwaves, and the firing of the meteor defense system into habitable land have permanently damaged Ringworld's environment.

LIFE ON RINGWORLD

The identity of the Ringworld Engineers is still a mystery. Many believe that the Pak created the ring as a place for their civilization to breed without inhibition or interference. However, the Pak never invented the gravity polarizer or other common

The Landscape of Ringworld   *The Guide to Larry Niven's Ringworld*

Known Space equipment, and it is unlikely that they could have discovered the secret to scrith and the other wonders of Ringworld, let alone keep from destroying themselves long enough to employ their new-found science.

Despite this, there is no doubt that other than the original Engineers, the Pak were the first race to inhabit the ring, bringing breeders from their homeworld in the galactic core. Mutations were destroyed and the Pak remained pure.

A virus killed off all the Protectors, and the breeders acquired genetic variability. Hominid races expanded, growing to fill every conceivable niche in Ringworld's ecology. Plant and animal life changed as well, bringing parasites, bacteria, and other undesirable aspects to a once idyllic garden. Many of the hominid races became genetic engineers and added to the inventory of life in attempts to eliminate disease. Exotic species like the Slaver sunflower flourish unchecked in many regions.

The total population of hominids on Ringworld is about thirty trillion.

And growing.

ENERGY AND POWER

The most common form of power on Ringworld is hard work. Hard work is normally generated through personal application, hiring others, or through slaves.

Sun, wind, and water are often harnessed by primitive civilizations in much the same way as on primitive Earth. Fossil fuels are extremely rare, since Ringworld never experienced a period where creatures died to become future sources of energy.

Alcohol is the most common artificial fuel, with crops used as the main source. Methane gas is also used by cultures centered around swamps and bogs. The Kzinti on the map of Kzin use hydrogen. There are many wood-driven railroads spanning the surface of the ring.

Most advanced cultures use the creations of the past to satisfy their energy requirements. Despite the superconductor plague, the power beamed back from the shadow squares is still accessible if a working receiving station can be found. Cultures like the Sea People have learned how to hook up lines to working sea dredges to power machinery in factories.

In general, any Ringworld civilization advanced enough to want a great deal of power has found some way to steal the energy from the engineers of the past. Though this is not necessarily a negative reflection on their society, it often means that the machinery takes on a near-mystical quality that prevents scientists and engineers from learning new scientific principles on their own.

THE ARCH

When darkness falls on Ringworld, an enormous parabolic Arch appears in the sky, attached to the vanishing edge of the Euclidean landscape. The ring stretches back over itself beyond the infinity plane with patches of alternating darkness and blue, becoming no more than a thin line of blue-white. The two Great Oceans are visible with the naked eye on either side of the ring, and sometimes the attitude jets fire, leaving candle-like phantoms in the air.

Many primitive cultures worship the ring as a covenant between the godlike Ringworld Engineers and man. Their altars depict a flat, disc-shaped landscape with blurred details surmounted by a parabolic arch. A highly polished golden ball representing the sun is suspended above the altar from "sunwire." The Arch is important to many aspects of these cultures, becoming part of their myth and psychology. In many cases, the City Builders encouraged worship of the Great Arch so the hominid races living beneath the remaining floating cities would continue to treat the City Builders as gods.

The Arch is an invaluable visual reference. Facing spinward, starboard is to the right and port to the left. It is easy for travelers to know when they are heading along the diameter of the ring or the width.

THE GREAT OCEANS

More than half of Ringworld's surface is water. When Ringworld was created, every region had enough water to sustain any number of life forms. The majority of the seas and oceans are about thirty feet deep, with more bays and coves than any civilization could ever use, designed by the Ringworld Engineers for boating and shipping. The coastlines never undergo extensive changes since the underlying material is immutable scrith.

The greatest bodies of water on Ringworld are the two Great Oceans, located on opposite sides of the ring. They are tremendously deep masses of saltwater whose areas are greater than two thousand times the surface of the Earth. The Great Oceans can be as deep as thirty-two kilometers, making the total volume of one ocean about twenty trillion cubic kilometers.

From the outer surface of Ringworld, the Great Oceans appear as deep bulges with infinite details of valleys, ridges, canyons, and peaks. Black triangular fins, hundreds of thousands of square kilometers in area act as heat sinks to cool the oceans. The scrith of the Great Oceans is especially thick to support the weight of the water and to ensure that meteor punctures do not leak the oceans into space.

The reason for the Great Oceans is a mystery. Though there are many equipment stockpiles and repair centers in the oceans, there seems to be no reason for such gigantic bodies of water to exist. There are many theories for their creation, such as the need for visual reference or "distraction to enemies," but none provide satisfactory explanations.

THE GREAT OVAL OCEAN AND THE GREAT STAR OCEAN

The Great Oval Ocean is roughly elliptical and is 1,360,000 kilometers long and 880,000 kilometers wide. The shoreline's length is easily thirty-two million miles, taking into account the myriad coasts and bays.

There are several large bays with areas equal to hundreds of planets. Tidal cycles are induced through hydrons, huge underwater flaps which force water masses to flow slowly into and out of these bays.

Several expeditions to Ringworld have explored some of the surface of the Great Oval Ocean. A dead City Builder urban center rests only 320,000 kilometers from the ocean, and Fist-of-God stands 160,000 kilometers from the ocean.

The Great Star Ocean is shaped like a ragged four pointed star and has never been explored.

MARINE LIFE AND STORMS

Marine life in the Great Oceans is too varied and profuse to catalog. There is a good majority of superstition about sea monsters; considering the size of the oceans and the wonder of Ringworld itself, there is little doubt that these tales are true. However, more common-sized life forms are known to exist, such as creatures which resemble sharks, killer whales, squid, Wunderland shadowfish, Gummidgy destroyers, and trapweed jungles. The Sea People are at least one known hominid species adapted to life in and near the ocean. There are also reports of sea Vampires.

The Great Oceans are so vast that the storms created in their depths are unimaginably powerful. Spiral-patterned storms like hurricanes are rare, but immense tidal waves that can build for hundreds of miles are not a myth.

THE ISLAND MAPS OF WORLDS

The most mysterious feature of the Great Oceans are the island maps of the worlds of space. Each is a full scale polar projection resting in the ocean. There are maps of Earth, Mars, Jinx, Down, Kzin, Kdat, Trinoc, and Pierin, in addition to other worlds known only by the Puppeteers. A map of the Puppeteer homeworld is not present.

The geological relationship of the land masses on the map of Earth suggest that the map's represented time is at least a quarter of a million years old; the map of Kzin seems to be slightly older. The maps are about 160,000 kilometers apart. Each map was originally stocked with the intelligent life form of the planet, as well as all the plant and animal species.

Like the oceans, the purpose of the maps is unknown. They may have been zoos or living transcripts of potentially hostile species. The map of Mars was used to hide one of the major control and repair centers.

CONDITIONS ON THE MAPS

The map of Earth was once populated by semi-sentient plains apes, or perhaps even Australopithecine species. However, explorers from the map of Kzin have taken the apes for slaves and food animals.

The map of Kzin is filled with primitive Kzinti before the interference of the Puppeteers; the female Kzinti are still intelligent. These Kzinti are fearless and actively explore the Great Oval Ocean. Their culture is ruled from the *Behemoth* (Interworld translation), a 1.6 kilometer-long ship driven by hydrogen power. They use chemical explosives in combat and fly hydrogen burning jet aircraft.

The map of Down is stocked with Grogs and no Kzinti has ever returned from an exploration mission. The map of Jinx has a channel through the middle, representing the banded ocean of the planet; any Bandersnatchi still living on the map can be found at the shores.

The maps of the non-terrestrial planets have never been explored. It is not known how the Trinoc's poisonous ecosystem is maintained, or how the Kdat world's heavier gravity is created.

THE MAP OF MARS AND THE CONTROL CENTER

The map of Mars hides one of Ringworld's major control and repair centers. The top of the map is twenty miles above sea level, and a huge waterfall runs around the rim to take the water vapor out of the atmosphere with condensers, since moist air is deadly to martians. Looking at the Great Oval Ocean from the outer surface of the ring, the indentation for the map of Mars is missing, suggesting that something is hidden.

There is a major nexus of the superconductor grid thirty-two kilometers beneath the pole of the map. A narrow scrith pillar leads to the main control complex, which is protected by a series of gigantic airlocks. The remaining space is a labyrinthine repair center with a volume of 4.48 billion cubic kilometers.

The repair center is a world built for Pak. Inside are power storage rings and fusion generators; tremendous heat exchangers and pumps cool the map of Mars. There are residences, a mile high exercise room, and a gigantic map room. Thousands of scrith repulsion disks are stored in tool sheds and lockers. Cavities around the perimeter of the map wall house equipment for repairing Ringworld's attitude jets, as well as one huge spacecraft. There are also hangar cavities that store Pak attack ships.

The repair center contains a smaller Pak environment area where the automatic controls for the meteor defense system are located, including manipulation of the superconductor grid and the subsystem that fires the meteor defense laser. The main ecosystem monitoring equipment, solar power collection controls, and spacecraft landing systems can also be controlled from this center.

In addition to living and storage space, the map of Mars also holds a 62.1 kilometer diameter hemispherical chamber used to grow tree-of-life. An artificial fusion sun lights the chamber, arcing slowly across the top of the dome to simulate night and day. Since the time of the map's construction, the garden has become wild with native Pak life forms from the galactic core. This dome is one of the most dangerous places on Ringworld: the smell of tree-of-life drives hominids mad.

Other repair centers may exist, but none have been discovered.

THE GREAT OVAL OCEAN

The Guide to Larry Niven's Ringworld   **The Landscape of Ringworld**

METEOR DEFENSE SYSTEM

Despite the strength of scrith, Ringworld is ironically vulnerable. Its completely artificial construction does not allow for natural rebalancing of the ecosystem. This means that a meteor striking the outer scrith could permanently damage the biosphere in a way where a normal planet might not have so great a problem. For example, enough meteor impacts could disturb the rotation of Ringworld about its sun.

The Ringworld Engineers swept the system clean of asteroids, planetoids, and comets to ensure that regular encounters with interstellar objects would not occur. However, space is filled with debris, and anything striking the outer scrith is probably traveling at thousands of miles per second. Even a spacecraft flying above the surface is an incredible threat to Ringworld; if a ship's drive fail for an instant, centrifugal force would drive it into the surface, killing millions of inhabitants.

To protect itself from interstellar harm, Ringworld is guarded by a gas laser capable of destroying just about anything (except a stasis field or scrith). The laser fires on targets the defense system determines is a threat, that is, something sufficiently large and moving on an intercept path with the inner surface of the ring; it also fires on anything moving 7.04 kilometers per second or faster. Upon detection, the superconductor grid magnetizes the scrith in the appropriate area on Ringworld, creating field-configurations strong enough to influence the direction of hydrogen-plasma streamers on the surface of the sun. The induced solar flares extrude to a length of several million kilometers (and about sixteen wide) in twenty minutes, at which time the hydrogen is made to lase.

The power of the laser is 3×10^{27} ergs/second, a small fraction of a normal sun's 4×10^{33} ergs/second total luminosity. Nonetheless, there is very little in Known Space that can withstand that kind of power. The defense system's controls are located in the Control Center beneath the Map of Mars in the Great Oval Ocean. The laser is programmed to fire on inhabited territory to protect the integrity of Ringworld; many of Ringworld's rising civilizations were cremated (such as the Healers) when they created MAGLEV vehicles capable of moving faster than 7.04 kilometers per second.

The tracking and targeting systems for the meteor defense system are located on the shadow squares. The system ignores anything incapable of harming the surface, such as small meteors that will burn up in the atmosphere before becoming a threat.

FOAMED SCRITH

Scrith is such an amazing substance that the Ringworld Engineers could change its "consistency." A foamed version of scrith was added to the outer surface of Ringworld to provide a passive meteor defense to stop any impacts that could not be stopped by the X-ray gas laser of the sun. The foamed scrith adds about a kilometer of depth to the normal scrith, filling in the contours and valleys that mark the terrain of the inner surface.

EYESTORMS AND PUNCTURES

Eyestorms are surreal and dangerous, brought to life by punctures in the Ringworld floor that have not been repaired by the automatic repair facilities. The puncture creates an air sink, and the atmosphere spews out into space, creating a partial vacuum. The lighter air from spinward tends to rise, while the heavier air from antispinward tends to fall since its rotational velocity is marginally increased with respect to Ringworld. The atmosphere creates a rolling hurricane that resembles a huge, disembodied eye. Eyestorms are white from clouds and blue from distance. The pupil of the eye is nearly black, lit by flashes of lightning.

The pupil is dangerous for flying vehicles to enter because of near gale-force winds; it is possible for a vehicle to be sucked down through the ring floor into deep space. However, the middle of the corridor created by the churning air is calm. Flying into this axis is like, "falling into the eye of God."

Weather patterns are disturbed for tens of thousands of square kilometers around an eyestorm. The air is always overcast and gloomy. The advantage to this is that Slaver sunflowers never grow in these regions and wind power is readily available. Many prosperous civilizations have grown under the baleful glare of eyestorms.

The original air circulation patterns set up by the Ringworld Engineers have long since been disrupted by numerous eyestorms. Fortunately, the overall loss of air is insignificant in comparison with the total volume, and the working repair and replenishment systems have easily compensated for the losses.

FIST-OF-GOD

Fist-of-God mountain towers on the median line a hundred thousand miles spinward from the oval Great Ocean. It is a 1,600 kilometers high, surrounded by a baked and barren desert. The earth and bedrock that cover the inner surface of Ringworld have been hurled away, leaving Fist-of-God's peak an edifice of bare scrith. The mountain tilts about ten degrees from the vertical, to antispinward, making its spinward slopes more gentle.

Fist-of-God was created when a moon-sized object struck the outer surface of Ringworld. The impact had the equivalent force of ten million trillion megatons, turning the moon to plasma and providing enough energy to deform the indestructible scrith floor. The blast was so strong that it was visible to both rims. It left a dead area around the mountain larger than the surface of the Earth. In addition, the impact forced the Great Ocean to drain and recede about thirteen kilometers to antispinward, leaving a salt-poisoned land in its wake.

The crater left at the top of the mountain juts out of the atmosphere of Ringworld. Its lip is a jagged line of damaged scrith, mountain-high, cold, and only a meter thick, stretched by the impact. The mountain is so high that no atmosphere spills out into space.

Fist-of-God's origins are a mystery, and many City Builder holo-tapes do not show its existence. Considering the age of the City Builder civilization, this puts Fist-of-God's age at about twelve centuries.

FLYCYCLES ENTER AN EYESTORM

SHADOW SQUARES AND SHADOW SQUARE WIRE

The inner surface of Ringworld is under constant sunlight. The Ringworld Engineers provided intervals of darkness by creating shadow squares, a chain of twenty black squares in orbit around Ringworld's sun at about the same distance as Mercury from the Earth. Each square is a 1.6 million kilometers wide and four million kilometers long; they are spaced 9.6 million kilometers apart. Their velocity is about 224 kilometers per second, rotating to provide a thirty hour day. This rotational velocity, combined with the rotation of Ringworld itself, results in nine hours of "night," and two forty-five minute periods of "twilight," which resemble total solar eclipses on Earth.

THE POWER OF THE SHADOW SQUARES

The Ringworld Engineers created the shadow squares for a second purpose. Each square is also a solar-thermoelectric converter whose energy is beamed back to the surface of Ringworld through microwave transmission. The shadow squares trap enormous amounts of energy equalling one-half percent of the sun's total output (the Earth traps less than a billionth of a percent of Sol's energy). The concentrated energy is about 2×10^{31} ergs/sec, which is fifty billion times more energy than created by the average terrestrial society.

The microwave transmitters of the shadow squares are infallible, but automatically shut down when not in use. The superconductor plague destroyed most of the receiving stations on Ringworld and caused a surface-wide power failure, resulting in the Fall of Cities.

OTHER USES OF THE SHADOW SQUARES

The Map Rooms of the City Builders employ the real-time holographic cameras mounted on the shadow squares. The shadow squares are also part of the meteor defense system, sliding back and forth to allow the X-ray laser to pass, constricting the ring of squares on the far side of the sun.

SHADOW SQUARE WIRE

Shadow square wire holds the ring of shadow squares together. The wire is nearly invisible because it is so thin, but it is also strong enough to cut through hullmetal (but not General Products hulls). Shadow square wire is immensely strong and remains solid at temperatures where most matter becomes plasma. Slaver disintegrators do not affect the wire; however, an X-ray laser would eventually melt it, and a shard of scrith could cut it.

The rotational speed of the shadow squares keeps the shadow square wire taut, and there is a mechanism in the squares to reel in and let out the wire to provide larger intervals between the squares for the meteor defense system. There is also a device (as yet unseen by Ringworld inhabitants) that replaces broken wire.

The original approach of the *Lying Bastard* (Louis Wu's first expedition ship) tore a length of shadow square wire from its socket. The wire eventually fell to the surface of Ringworld. Appearing as a cloud of thin black smoke, it shrouded a city and eventually cut it to dust.

NOTES ON SHADOW SQUARE WIRE

The properties of shadow square wire resemble that of scrith so closely, there is little doubt that they are the same substance. If the Ringworld Engineers had the ability to form scrith into something as unbelievably massive as Ringworld, they could form it into something infinitesimally small.

RIM WALLS

The tremendous spin of Ringworld would normally force the atmosphere into space, leaving the surface airless within a few years. The Ringworld Engineers built walls at the rim of the ring, high enough to ensure that the air would not be lost. The rim walls are 1,600 kilometers high and rise in the direction of the sun. Any leaks are easily replaced by the atmosphere replenishment system.

The majority of the atmosphere lies below the thirty-five mile mark of the rim walls. The walls are sculpted into the shapes and textures of mountains. In the places between the mountains, the rim wall is a smooth, glassy, cliff that cannot be scaled. The top of the rim wall is only about thirty meters across, and the bare scrith has been textured to ensure safe foot-holds. There is no detail on the spaceward side of the rim wall.

The rim wall and rim wall mountains are barely visible from the median line of Ringworld, located at the "horizon" line. Traveling toward the wall creates the illusion that the height of the wall seems to decrease, as if standing at the rounded corner of a fortress whose walls recede away at ninety degree angles to one another.

Deep-radar will not penetrate the rim wall, and stepping discs do not function through the scrith.

THE SPILL MOUNTAINS

The spill mountains are part of Ringworld's recycling system. There are 47,760 mountains spaced at roughly 66° on each rim. They are fifty to sixty kilometers high and appear to be near-regular half-cones leaning against the rim walls. The spill mountains are smoothly weathered and "terra-formed" in half circles: dirty peaks followed by ice and snow giving way to rocky foothills. The lowest slopes have glaciers of ice and permafrost, and there is a constant cover of fog at the mountains' bases.

Ringworld has no counterbalance to erosion, which means that the topsoil would be stripped from the plains, carried away by winds and rivers in a few thousand years. The Ringworld Engineers anticipated the damaging effect of erosion, placing huge dredges in the sea and ocean floors to keep the sludge flowing. This "flup" is forced down heated drainpipes and through the ring floor, where other pipes circulate the flup up the rim walls. Dust is sprayed out into the atmosphere to settle back onto the plains, and the sludge is deposited on the top of the spill mountains, where it finds its way back to the biosphere, continuously regenerating the soil. The moisture in the flup is boiled away and turned to vapor and ice.

THE SPILL MOUNTAINS AND THE SUPERCONDUCTOR PLAGUE

The Ringworld Engineers planned for every contingency except for the ring-wide loss of power created by the Puppeteer superconductor plague. This caused the shadow squares to cease their power transmissions, which in turn shut down many of the automatic dredges in the rivers and seas, creating huge bogs and swamps in some areas and arid deserts in others.

Less than a third of the spill mountains continue to operate since the flow of flup has been interrupted. The remainder have insubstantial flows which cannot make up for failure of the other mountains. Unless the flow is restarted, Ringworld's environment will be irrevocably damaged.

THE SPILL MOUNTAIN FOLK

The Spill Mountain Folk are a hominid species adapted to living in the cold and high altitude of the mountains. Their cities are built into the vertical slopes of ice on the mountains, interconnected by walkways and suspension bridges. They rely on balloons for transportation.

The Spill Mountain Folk were allied with the City Builders before the superconductor plague. The Folk did the majority of the work on the rim transport system, and also ran the elevator tubes and spaceports.

SPILL MOUNTAINS AND RIM WALL SECTION

The Landscape of Ringworld

The Guide to Larry Niven's Ringworld

SPACECRAFT LANDING SYSTEM

Landing a ship on Ringworld is not easy. The ring's rotation of 1,232 kilometers/second could take a fusion drive ship days or weeks to build up the proper velocity, but there is the additional problem of angular momentum that must be taken into account; a ship must keep moving along the line of Ringworld, which is curved, and therefore must apply an appropriate amount of thrust for the angle. In addition, any ship approaching the ring falls under the dangerous scrutiny of the meteor defense system.

The Ringworld Engineers compensated for these needs by creating the spacecraft landing system, a series of immense toroids about sixteen kilometers in diameter affixed to the outer surface of the ring. These rings form an electromagnetic cannon, a linear accelerator consisting of hundreds of rings extending for hundreds of thousands of kilometers. There are six of these landing systems situated on the outer ring surface, each 60° from the other.

City Builder holotapes illustrate the operation of the landing system. A ship falls into the ring's orbit but does not try to match the ring's velocity. The ship situates itself eighty kilometers from the base of the rim wall on the axis of the accelerator. As the toroids sweep past, the ship is gradually accelerated to match speeds with the ring.

The toroids glow with pastel colors, enabling operators to track incoming ships and monitor feedback systems. The spaceports are on the sunward side of the landing edges, 110 kilometer shelves far past the end of the accelerator. Kilometer long cradles wait in rows for incoming ramships, and cranes once fitted ships for expeditions. There are crawlers and equipment stockpiles littered throughout the spaceport ledges, well-preserved in the vacuum. Cziltang brones also wait in the cold of space.

The spaceport launching facility was little more than a huge hatch and a catapult for ejecting ships into space. Ships leaving Ringworld had enough speed to escape the gravity well and start their fusion ramscoops.

ATTITUDE JETS

Ringworld is unstable in the plane of its orbit. Meteor strikes or solar flares could throw the ring off balance. The attitude jets ensure that Ringworld retains its equilibrium in the same way that the spokes on a bicycle keep the rim centered.

Each rim wall holds two hundred jets spaced at 1.8° intervals, about 4.8 million kilometers apart; one hundred and twenty spill mountains lie between each jet. The jets are Bussard ramjets that collect hydrogen from the solar wind in a 6.5 to 8 thousand kilometer radius, meaning that the attitude jets never run out of fuel. They are one thousand five hundred foot toroids mounted on fifty mile towers which seemed to be stretched out of the rim wall scrith.

The jets create "ghost flames" when they fire sunward, a term used by many of the hominid species on the inner surface of the ring to describe the luminous, violet flames. Further jets appear as candle flames in the sky.

THE CITY BUILDERS AND THE ATTITUDE JETS

The City Builders, believed to be the most advanced race on Ringworld, never developed hyperdrive or gravity polarizers. When they discovered cziltang brones, they were able to leave the inner surface of the ring and travel to the outer edge, beginning their golden age of interstellar travel. They traveled at relativistic speeds and took boosterspice to increase their life-spans.

Unfortunately, the City Builders took the easy path to exploration, and instead of building their own ships, dismantled many of the attitude jets and turned them into giant fusion ramships. These ships are the largest in Known Space, eight hundred feet in diameter and over a mile long. The ships had their own reentry and return vehicles for planetary landings; the ramships themselves carried thousands of passengers, spinning to induce artificial gravity and at the same time creating a magnetic field reversal effect which shielded the ship from the stream of incoming hydrogen ions.

The City Builders' passion for discovery once put Ringworld in jeopardy of falling off-axis into the sun. Only the intervention of Louis Wu and his companions saved the ring.

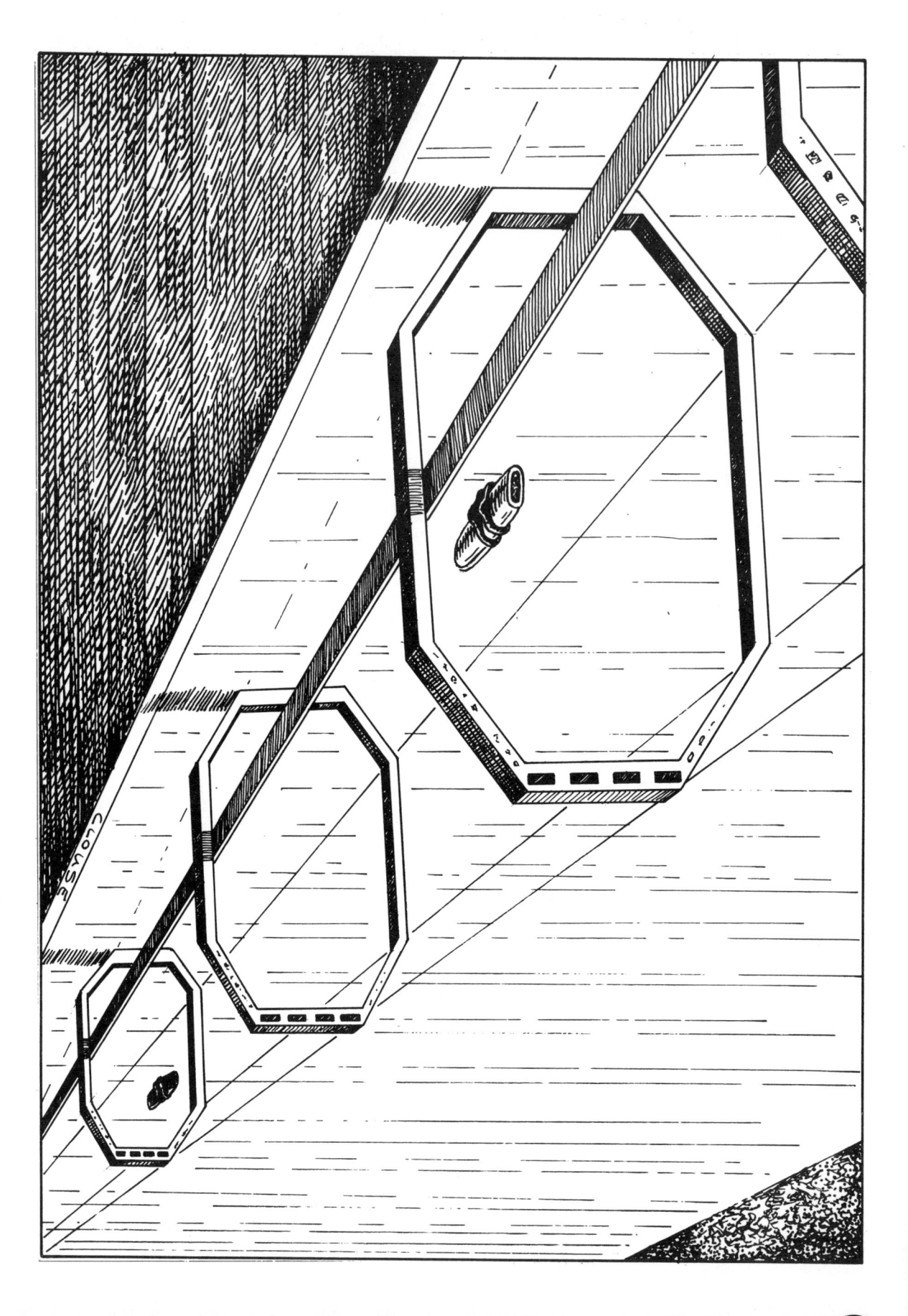

SPACECRAFT LANDING SYSTEM

The Guide to Larry Niven's Ringworld — *The Landscape of Ringworld*

RIM TRANSPORT SYSTEM

The rim transport system is a creation of the City Builders using the electromagnetic principles so prevalent in every aspect of their technology. Like the spacecraft landing system, the transport system is an electromagnetic cannon, a series of toroids that accelerate, then decelerate, a transport vehicle along the outer rim of the ring. The system was so fast that any point on the rim wall could be reached within fourteen days. The toroids of the transport system were much smaller than the ones of the spacecraft landing system, only sixty meters in diameter.

Except for short distances, the shuttles always traveled anti-spinward, employing the ring's incredible rotational speed to allow the shuttle to "coast" to its destination. The shuttles are fifty-eight meters long and nine meters in diameter, roomy and comfortable with oversized windows.

Work on the rim transport system slowed when the City Builders began their mass expeditions into space. The network of toroids covers forty percent of the starboard rim wall, and only fifteen percent of the port (the zero median line runs through the pole of the map of Mars).

City Builder culture tended to grow around the bases of the rim walls, where elevators could take passengers to the transport system. Segments of the system were built farther away on the wall of the ring, near the attitude jet towers; these systems were used when the attitude jets were being removed for use in the City Builder ramships.

A good number of the rim transport system toroids continue to operate, having escaped the superconductor plague.

RACES OF THE RINGWORLD

127	CITY BUILDERS
139	GHOULS
142	GRASS GIANTS
145	HAIRY ONES
147	HANGING PEOPLE
149	HEALERS
151	HERDERS
153	MACHINE PEOPLE
155	MUD PEOPLE
157	SEA PEOPLE
159	VAMPIRES

CITY BUILDERS

The City Builders conjured Ringworld's shining era of fairy-tale cities and fabulous technologies. They profoundly influenced dozens of other hominid species with two hundred centuries of scientific, social, and political achievements. City Builder explorations were courageous, leading to unending wonder. As far as it is known, they are the only race of Ringworld to reach the spaceports and travel between the stars.

The development of City Builder civilization is a mystery. They often drew on the technologies of other species in all areas of social and scientific advance. Their own experiments were remarkably dangerous, and many of them not well planned. The loss of the Ringworld attitude jets is an example of their lack of foresight.

EXPLORING THE RING

City Builders developed Ring-cartography and mapped patterns of the Superconductor grid in the Ringworld foundation. They used simple magnets to determine that there was a web-work of lines running in 80,000 kilometer hexes through the foundation of the Ringworld. They discovered that the web-work was the same everywhere, regularly intersecting the Spill Mountains.

It took generations before the City Builders learned enough physics to understand what they'd been mapping. Their speculations led to the creation of their own superconductors, followed by magnetic fusion power, beamed microwave energy, and Magnetic Levitation (MAGLEV) scrith-repulsion transportation systems. The pinnacle of the City Builders' rise to power was the discovery of the solar power generated by the shadow squares. When they tapped into the collector stations located at the superconductor grid intersections, they had a near-infinite energy resource.

ESCAPING THE RING

When they reached the outer rim-wall spaceports, the City Builders found abandoned spaceports with stockpiles of bulk material, in addition to a few vehicles, winches, and unrecognizable pieces of equipment which they eventually learned created an osmosis-inducing field that temporarily rendered scrith permeable to matter. They named the devices *cziltang brones*, and with them were able to drag through sufficient quantities of parts, equipment, and crews to man the spaceport.

The City Builders also discovered huge fusion ramships, primitive, but serviceable. The ships' ramscoop-field generators were of the same design as the attitude jet toroids. The City Builders dismounted many of the Ringworld's attitude-jets to create their starship ramscoops; the design of the attitude jets fixed the dimensions of the City Builder ramships. They learned of the meteor defense system the hard way.

The stage was set for a golden age of interstellar exploration and colonization. The immense City Builder ramships were flung clear of the Ringworld by its 1,232 kilometer per second spin. The huge electromagnetic loops of the spacecraft decelerator were used by returning to ships to match velocities with the Ringworld for landing.

City Builder expeditions naturally headed for the stars, since the system of Ringworld had been swept entirely clear of planets and other debris by the Engineers. There is little doubt that the ancient City Builders thought that the idea of spherical worlds was strange; they may have discovered information on normal planets through holograms left behind by the Ringworld Engineers.

A typical interstellar flight followed a loop 300 light years long, covering five or six Earthlike worlds in four solar systems. Only a few dozen years of ship-time would pass for the crew and passengers before their return to the Ringworld, but their own cultures sometimes changed enormously in these intervals. The City Builders knew of, and may have explored and partially terraformed some of the habitable planets in human space. Earth may have been used as a base for a time. The total volume traversed by the ramships is thought to be hundreds of times greater than the volume of Known Space. Traveling was subject to relativistic time-dilation, so the City Builders supplied their ramship crews with a longevity drug much more powerful than boosterspice.

There may still be thousands of City Builder ramships traveling through space with exotic cargos. Their logs and destinations were lost during the superconductor plague.

The Guide to Larry Niven's Ringworld   **Races of the Ringworld**

THE CITY BUILDER EMPIRE

The City Builders were the undisputed masters of a large section of Ringworld. The citizens of their empire outnumbered the current human population in Known Space. Hundreds of thousands of cities flourished, floating high above the ground through MAGLEV field-generators that drew power beamed directly to the shadow-square solar energy receiver stations. Many of the metropolises were extensive lines of skyscrapers and urban centers. They were all rich sources of social and economic power, as well as centers of military might and political influence; they were the hubs of City Builder society, as well as monuments to the races' domination of the Ringworld.

Each city had its own aesthetic, though they all shared many traits of style with other floating cities. Buildings were shaped as simple solids, such as cylinders or cones, or geometric shapes like tetrahedrons. The exteriors were rarely decorated by anything more than the most simple ornamentation. The white, stone-like construction material of a city was uniformly colored, though slight variation in hue was common. The silent machinery of the floating cities was unobtrusive and self-repairing.

The floating cities were the homes of the City Builder elite, where the administrative, cultural, and political regimes were separated from the ground dwelling hominids. The cities were also the centers of technological and social advances, as well as the highest courts of law and top security prisons. Military and police installations had armories filled with laser and electromagnetic weapons rarely used by any but the City Builders themselves.

The greatest libraries and centers for learning were also contained within the floating walls. There was a great deal of information concerning the myths and histories of the City Builders and all the hominid species under their control. Records of ramship journeys and exploration of the Ringworld could be easily found on public viewing machines. The top of every library contained the public Map Room, where the sensors located on the Shadow Squares created a huge holographic projection of every detail of the Ringworld.

Malls and markets were an integral part of the richness of City Builder society. Everything from bizarre pets to rishathra perfume could be found at the market. There were also auditoriums, spas, banquet halls, convention centers, and all other places of social repast. The most luxurious apartments were located near the

A FLOATING METROPOLIS OF THE CITY BUILDER EMPIRE

top of the floating cities; the sky-castles of the rulers were also found in the city.

THE CITIES
Each beautiful metropolis was autonomous, though not self-sufficient. Cities were often built as far apart as the Earth is from the Moon. Gigantic MAGLEV aircraft and the rim transport system linked the empire and provided a means to travel to the farthest reaches of the Ringworld. Equally important were the microwave beam transmitters used for communication which allowed the City Builders to exchange information over the great distances between their cities. Map Room images were of paramount importance to extremely distant regions.

Each isolated metropolis was the regional government, orchestrating the affairs of a state larger than the surface area of the Earth. Rulers were often the most powerful of the City Builder families, their allies, and loyal servants. City Builder government was not a matter of force of arms, but rule through wisdom, satisfying the needs of the subjects through shrewd economic manipulation and careful management of information and religions. The City Builders most likely created the worship of the Arch in the more primitive hominids.

THE CITIES BELOW
Thousands of roads ran beneath the floating cities, connecting the vast seas of ground-dwellings in a staggering web which extended for thousands of square kilometers; cities like these standing on shorelines surrounded entire seas the size of the Mediterranean. Traders and non-City Builder hominids were the most common inhabitants of the cities beneath the floating cities. The cities themselves were centers of culture for hundreds of different species. Many of these species worked directly with the City Builders and were welcome to live in the floating cities, but much of the metropolises were off limits. The hominids usually performed menial tasks and services.

Like the floating cities, the ground-based cities were often clustered around a central point. The main structures were tall spires rising above a continuous mass of smaller buildings. A few of the spires would sometimes reach the bottoms of the floating cities. Also like the floating cities, the ground based dwellings were designed around simple geometric structures, though the influence of local hominid cultures sometimes affected the details of the city.

Unlike the floating cities, the ground cities were heavily populated, except for the areas where the floating castles cast permanent shadows (the fungus farms were located in this darkness). The aesthetic of the City Builders as a culture prevented them from creating mundane recreation parks or fields. They preferred crowded amphitheaters and public squares, malls, shops, public baths, hanging gardens, practically anything where masses of people might gather to converse or trade.

Many of the urban districts were built to accommodate a particular hominid species. The rule of the City Builders was so strong that there was no prejudice or bigotry among the various races.

RISHATHRA

The City Builder term for sex with a partner of a different hominid species is *rishathra*, a widely known cultural remnant of the City Builder's rise to power. Many species on Ringworld continue to use rishathra as a means of birth control or a way to create a truce or finalize an agreement. It is often performed happily with a great deal of ritual.

The City Builders studied rishathra, mastering it when they discovered its power over the less-sophisticated kingdoms. They produced detailed archives and reference materials showing the preferences and limitations of the hominid species. Other information included preferred positions, taboos, and aggression.

Many pacts were made with visiting dignitaries through rishathra and gifts of the City Builder longevity drug, the most powerful and valuable in Known Space. A potent tool for political control emerged when super-pheromone vampire-scent was refined for use as "rishathra perfume." Some of the hominids who were subservient to the City Builders became addicted and dependent.

Different species have varying attitudes about rishathra, and there are many strict rules that follow its use, especially about who suggests its use and who must perform it. Some races who value their fertility do not allow the practice, while others are physiologically or biochemically prohibited from inter-species sex.

THE CROWDED LANDSCAPE OF THE CITIES BELOW

Rishathra is not always voluntary, especially with some of the Ringworld hominids who are immune or intolerant of the vampire-perfume. Many times, young City Builders are forced to perform rishathra to pay debts before they are allowed to begin their own families.

Some civilizations use rishathra to promote their holdings in the same way as the City Builders. There are many complex rituals surrounding this use of rishathra, but the origins of the practice have vanished with the fall of the ancient City Builder society.

CITY BUILDER APPEARANCE

City Builders are slim and aristocratic, taller than the average human but rarely rising over two meters. Their ghostly pale flesh is unknown to any other race in Known Space. They have a small nose and nearly no lips, and neither sex has facial hair, including eyebrows. The skull is finely shaped and delicate.

The top of the City Builders' heads are bald except for a fringe just above the ears. Normal hair grows below this point, thick and lustrous and black, often longer than shoulder length. The City Builder fashion is to throw this hair forward from the shoulder.

The eyes of a City Builder are hypnotic and penetrating, and often unsettling. Their expressions are difficult to read, especially by people unfamiliar with the race. City Builders rarely smile and have an air of extreme austerity.

City Builders live with other hominids for short periods of time and are usually treated as gods. The unsophisticated hominids of Ringworld take the City Builders to be holy images incarnate, views to the past of a time when castles floated in the sky and miracles were a daily occurrence.

While traveling, City Builders are most likely to have technical knowledge and equipment greater than any other race on the Ringworld.

*AN AUSTERE CITY BUILDER
CONTEMPLATES THE MARVELS OF HIS RACE*

At the same time that the last American colony was established in Georgia, a plague that destroyed superconductors ravaged the Ringworld and the lives of the City Builders. The devastation was a plot by the Puppeteers to increase their trade with minimal risk. The Experimentalist Hindmost government purchased the location of the Ringworld from the Outsiders; telescopes, robotic probes, and spectrographs analyzed the Ringworld structure and discovered the superconductor grid embedded in the scrith. The Puppeteers created a technophytic bacterium that fed on superconductor material. The robotic probes were then sent to spread the plague across the Ringworld, with the plan that the Puppeteer trading ships would follow, bringing costly aid to the hapless citizens.

However, a Conservative faction took control of the Puppeteer government before the plan could be completed. The new faction decided that the Ringworld was too great a risk for the Puppeteers to exploit and the project was abandoned.

THE EFFECTS OF THE SUPERCONDUCTOR PLAGUE

The City Builders could not find the reason for the superconductor breakdown. The majority of their machinery broke down. When the solar-power receiver stations failed, the tremendous energy-beams which sustained most of the MAGLEV flotation units and transportation systems shut down. The decreased energy requests automatically shut down the shadow square thermoelectric generators so that they provided no additional power that could have been picked up by emergency stations.

Cziltang brones failed while crews were making their way through the scrith. Many of the crews were trapped in the scrith and died instantly, while the rest were stranded at the spaceport ledges, unable to get back because there was no direct, physical link between the ledges and the rest of the Ringworld.

The magnificent, dream-like cities of the City Builders smashed to the ground, taking billions of lives. Urban centers on the ground below were demolished by the falling towers, driving tall buildings through the lower levels of the floating castles. Huge seafarms and marine metropolises drawing their primary energy from the beams sank beneath the water; ships and air-shuttles met disaster.

Continent-sized sandstorms buried cities where seas had

dried. Other metropolises were flooded by silt-blocked rivers and streams, and Ringworld's first swamps formed where there was too much water in the grasslands.

The City Builders' civilization collapsed overnight.

THE REMAINS OF THE CITIES

A handful of the floating buildings with sealed, independently-operating power sources survived. Great libraries remain with their histories of exploration and intraspecies civilization intact. There are also mythic and epic adventures, and records of incredible ramship voyages stored on book-tape archives in banks of public reading machines. Map Rooms still function where there is power.

Generations of looting and vandalism have destroyed a good portion of anything that survived the original catastrophe, while trees and vines have done their best to bring down the remaining buildings. Many places became the homes of animals, bandits, or more insidious creatures, such as Vampires.

Ringworld natives in many regions still use the old City Builder tongue, or dialects derived from it. Those that live in the shadow of the once great City Builder cities are usually descended from City Builder genes, with similar features. Intermediate-level industrial cultures avidly seek out technological artifacts buried in long forgotten City Builder ruins. Some primitive hominids revere the City Builders as a race of vanished gods.

It has been discovered that some of the City Builder artifacts are still operational. Examples of these are security systems that had independent power sources, such as the police speed-trap fields originally set to keep vehicles from traveling too quickly in the floating cities. These units burn out drive units and other circuits, and often draw the offending vehicle into a holding facility for arrest. In addition, many communication frequencies were limited to police, military, and government use. Some portable communications systems found on the Ringworld might violate these frequencies and attract the attention of functioning police scanners, resulting in the destruction of the equipment.

THE REMNANTS OF THE ONCE GREAT CITY BUILDER EMPIRE

GHOULS

Ghoul is the more common name for the Night People. Their main roles in the Ringworld ecology are scavengers and information gatherers. They often approach friendly villages to collect their share of edible garbage. In other areas they bear away the bodies of the dead, and attack settlements who bury or cremate their dead until they change their ways.

The society of the Night People is spread far across the Ringworld. They have gained an awareness of the dimensions of their home. Ghouls are reasonably peaceful and reasonably tolerated, showing no propensity for intrusion. They know the religious ceremonies and customs of thousands of cultures, accepting their place with fatalistic acceptance.

"The activities of other species rarely interfere with our own lives, and in the end they all belong to us," is a common Ghoul phrase.

INFORMATION TO SELL

The most important role of the Night People is the accumulation and sale of valuable information they gather on their scavenging throughout the Ringworld. They find myth and rumor of equal use to actual fact, but do not antagonize other species through manipulation. Ghouls rarely understand the implications of the events they see or the information they sell.

The undocumented information, legends, and visual impressions of the Ghouls are often as valuable as actual scientific fact. The City Builders, Machine People, and similar societies have a great deal of respect for the Night People that goes far beyond normal tolerance. The Ghouls are often given access to libraries to expand on their already considerable base of information in the hopes that other facts will be revealed at another time.

The Ghouls have a system of long-range information exchange through the use of large mirrors which they use to speak with the Spill Mountain Folk. However, the details of their complete communication network remains a mystery.

THE WAY OF THE GHOULS

The Ghouls are not interested in changing their way of life. They occasionally gain access to sophisticated technology, but do little more than hoard the ancient books and relics they collect.

They are comfortable with their nocturnal life-style and wise enough to understand its limitations, rarely stepping beyond its bounds.

PHYSIOLOGY

Ghouls appear to be a horrid cross between a human and a jackal. They are equally comfortable moving on all fours as standing erect, though they always walk upright when in the cities of advanced societies.

Night People are smaller than humans, rarely reaching 1.5 meters tall. Their skin coloration is a combination of dark purple and charcoal, covered by iron-gray or black fur. Their fur traps the stench of their nocturnal life-style and their breath is truly formidable.

A Ghoul's hands and feet end in sharp claws, and their mouths are filled with wedge-shaped teeth, excellent for ripping. Their ears are large and sensitive, resembling goblin ears. Their large, brown eyes are unsettlingly human and their vision is excellent.

THE GHOUL PROTECTOR

There is one known Ghoul who ate tree-of-life root and became a Protector. She assisted the Teela Brown Protector in repairing the Ringworld's attitude jets. She also helped in the evacuation of the breeders from the lands threatened by radiation.

A GHOUL INSPECTS THE TREASURES OF THE NIGHT

GRASS GIANTS

Grass Giants are a race of huge humanoid herbivores living in the veldts of Ringworld. Their war parties march out of their grass covered longhouses to attack any herbivores, carnivorous species herding meat-animals, or other enemies who threaten their forage areas. They are fearsome and confident.

GRASS GIANT SOCIETY

Grass Giants have a herdlike society led by a king, who is the dominant male of the tribe. The other Grass Giants are subservient to the king, but have their own hierarchy of most dominant to least dominant. Like the Kzinti, the Grass Giants wear the scars of battle as signs of strength, and, in fact, have many of the domineering personality traits of the Kzinti. However, Grass Giants are not foolish enough to attack an obviously superior enemy.

The king is often the target of frequent challenges, so he is usually the biggest and strongest of the tribe. He remains king only so long as he defeats challengers.

Female Grass Giants are always subservient to the males, but maintain their own social order. Frequent sexual attention usually conveys higher status. For the most part, female Grass Giants are efficient at organizing and establishing routines but show little imagination.

Grass Giants meet insults to their honor with great ferocity. They are especially intolerant of other races who comment that the Giants must be docile because they eat plants instead of meat.

GRASS GIANTS AND RISHATHRA

Only the Grass Giant king gets to officially mate with the females. There are times when the king goes on holiday, leaving plenty of time for the rest of the tribe to get on with their much-needed business. When the king returns, play-time's over.

Grass Giant males go out of their way to practice rishathra, proving their superior masculinity to other Ringworld hominids whenever possible. The species uses rishathra to seal pacts and treaties.

The structure of their society means Grass Giants do not tolerate much of Known Space's views of sexual equality.

The Guide to Larry Niven's Ringworld *Races of the Ringworld*

LIFE ON THE VELDT

Grass Giant tribes require huge amounts of forage each day; they seldom remain in a single area for very long since the food supplies quickly run low. Their temporary homes are made of mud and grass with reinforced vertical supports constructed from trees. The longhouse is the main building of the village, a dirt-floored structure four meters high used for communal shelter, ritual, and weapons storage.

The Grass Giants prefer to sleep in huge naked piles with the king in the center surrounded by heaps of women. Fifty to five hundred more males and females sleep in the area around their king. They always post guards and send out night patrols for security.

APPEARANCE

Grass Giants are about the same size as Kzinti, though the Grass Giant king is usually larger, about three meters tall. Their skin and eyes are brown, and they are covered with masses of yellow hair, not so much bearded as maned. Both males and females go naked.

Grass Giant war parties contain forty or more warriors, heavily armed and armored, led by the king.. They typically carry huge swords or halberds, wearing plate armor on their arms and legs. The king wears a specially made suit of armor that covers his entire body, though he leaves the faceplate open.

The king's armor resembles the appearance of a Pak Protector.

GRASS GIANTS AND SLAVER SUNFLOWERS

The Grass Giants use Slaver sunflowers to protect the longhouses. They grow the "fire plants" on the sod of the longhouse's roof; it is almost impossible to out-move a sunflower.

A GRASS GIANT PLANTS HIS SLAVER SUNFLOWERS

HAIRY ONES

Hairy One is a term used to describe any regressive City Builder species living near the remains of floating cities. Hairy Ones are omnivorous farmers, domesticating animals and tending plots. They rarely use machinery and never develop technologies on their own; they don't even build their own houses, living in the remains of cities.

The Hairy Ones think of themselves as civilized. They long for a return to the old days of glory when people lived in castles in the sky. They do nothing to speed this process and are willing to wait for the City Builders to return to do the job for them.

Religion among the Hairy Ones is confined to a single ideal. They believe that the City Builders constructed the world and raised the Great Arch (the upward curve of the Ringworld on the horizon line) as a sign of Holy Covenant. They call the City Builders "Engineers."

APPEARANCE

Hairy Ones have pale white skin and are almost completely covered by tightly-curled ash-blonde hair. Beards cover the males' faces, revealing only their soft brown eyes. They average between five and six feet tall and have extraordinarily long fingers.

There is very little remarkable about the Hairy Ones except for their seemingly complex religions that have been the bane of many Ringworld travelers.

THE HAIRY ONES WORSHIP THE ARCH

HANGING PEOPLE

Hanging People are small hominids who live in the upper branches of jungle and forest trees. They rarely leave their homes and serve as the protectors of the plant and animal life in their region.

There are many races of Hanging People and they breed gregariously, being found in every part of the Ringworld. When they travel, they sell their services as technicians and precision electronics experts; they are adept at their professions and are expensive.

The more adventuresome of the Hanging People can be hired as thieves and burglars. They are often more intrigued by the difficulty of the caper than the promise of payment.

APPEARANCE

Hanging People are arboreal vegetable eaters who average about a meter tall. They have elongated human-sized heads that seem wrong for their light body frames. Their arms, legs, fingers, and toes are slender; they have opposable first toes and thumbs. Their sense of touch is so remarkable that it is said rishathra with them is unbelievably satisfying.

Hanging People are covered by fine, silky hair ranging from forest green through yellow-green to shades of orange and brown, with occasional markings and discolorations. Hanging People in oceanic or tropical regions sometimes have blue or bright yellow fur.

When traveling in mixed company, Hanging People wear light, brightly-colored gowns. They are not aggressive but often act temperamental and reserved.

TROPICAL HANGING ONES BASK IN THE SUNLIGHT

HEALERS

Many hominid species on the Ringworld rose and fell due to their own pride, usually when they created magnetic repulsion vehicles that caught the attention of the meteor defense system. The race known as the Healers is among them.

The Healers' civilization also came into conflict with the City Builders, who used the heavy weaponry discovered at the Ringworld spaceports to destroy the Healers and steal their considerable knowledge. However, the Healers are widespread throughout the Ringworld, slowly and secretly rebuilding the remains of their glory.

Healers have a reputation among the hominid races as being, "magicians without armor," healing the sick and curing the deformed. Before the original destruction of their lives, the Healers used their extensive knowledge of biochemistry and similar sciences to cleanse the environment that had caused so many mutations and diseases in the Ringworld ecology. They now carry this knowledge on their lone travels through their predesignated superconductor hexagonal regions, helping everyone who requires aid.

APPEARANCE

The Healers are usually over two meters tall and have well-developed bodies. Their skin is colored like reddish straw which darkens to rust brown in the sun. Their rich auburn hair grows over the top and sides of the head, and down their backs to the base of spine.

Healers have longer heads than humans with long ears and narrow cheekbones. Their features often appear brooding and striking. Their black, hazel, or blue eyes are deep set and occasionally slanted.

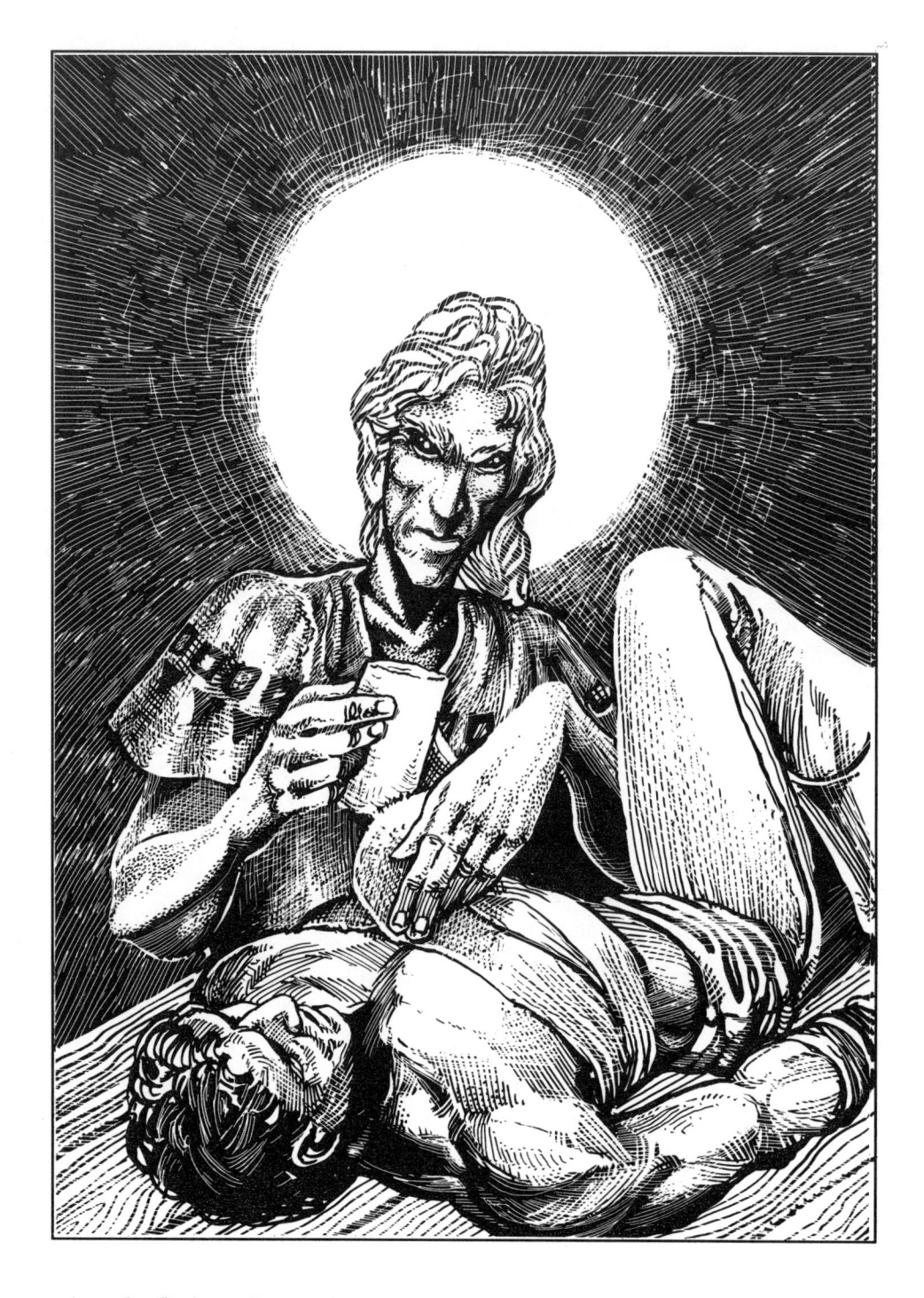

A CONCERNED HEALER TENDS A WOUNDED PATIENT

HERDERS

The Herders are small red carnivorous hominids who live in the plains and tend their herds of meat-animals. There are dozens of Herder tribes who all refer to themselves as "the People." Each tribe herds a different animal, which they eat freshly killed and uncooked.

Herders are extremely fast and are able to bound through high grass with amazing speed; however, there is little chance that they could outrun a Kzin. They use nothing more than simple spears and nets, and have never developed sophisticated technology of their own.

The tribes like visitors, who bring the opportunity to have a "trading feast" where there is a chance to swap goods and exchange stories. Out of disinterest, no known Herder tribe practices rishathra.

APPEARANCE

Herders are short and lean, humanlike but never exceeding a meter and a half in height. Their skin is uniformly red and they are hairless except for rusty colored hair curling over their scalps.

Herders have excellent vision and hearing. Their eyes are small and black, and their ears are rounded and stand out from the head. Their teeth are so pointed they look as if they are filed.

The language of the Herders is a series of high-pitched squeaks. Their voices are childlike falsettos.

Elder Herders wear kilts of decorated leather. The rest of the tribes wear whatever clothing pleases them.

HERDERS RUN AFTER THEIR PREY

The Guide to Larry Niven's Ringworld — Races of the Ringworld

MACHINE PEOPLE

The empire of the Machine People is an example of the types of civilizations that rise up around the floating City Builder cities that have been pieced together from buildings with isolated power sources. The Machine People believe that they trade with the City Builders out of logical choice and maintain the floating city out of tradition. They do not suspect the true political and technological power of the City Builders; a war would no doubt be devastating for both races.

The Machine People's empire is several hundred-thousand square kilometers in area, centered around a floating city. Resources are extremely limited and they are forced to use strip-mining and reclamation to obtain the materials necessary to expand their civilization. The Machine People empire's greatest problem is the diversity of the cultures within it and the conflicts that occur, such as between the herbivorous Grass Giants and the animal-tending Herders.

The Machine People have developed most of their technology on their own, with little help from the City Builders. Their equipment is usually heavy and sturdy without concern for aesthetics. Machine People buildings are short and wide, made of concrete and similar construction materials. They sometimes take great journeys to abandoned cities in search of artifacts.

Coincidentally, the Machine People have a major problem with alcoholism since much of their power comes from natural fuels.

APPEARANCE

Machine People look like widened humans, stocky and muscular, standing no more than 1.8 meters tall. Their skin has a dark olive tone and their eye color is usually blue, green, brown, or dark orange. Men and women have a fringe of fine black hair running along the lower jaw.

Machine People dress simply and wear little adornment. The eldest of the society might wear something brighter than the usual browns and blues of everyday work clothes.

ONE OF THE MACHINE PEOPLE DISCOVERS SOMETHING IN THE RUINS

MUD PEOPLE

The Mud People are shunned by other races for several very important reasons, the most important of which is known as the Age of Transformation. A genetic virus attacks two thirds of the Mud People population, just after the Age of Breeding passes, transforming the victims into hideous Muck Ogres. All Mud People are carriers and it is suspected that the virus can attack other hominids as well, suggesting that the virus originates with the Pak Breeders. None of the younger Mud People believes that the virus will afflict them. When the virus strikes, there is a rise in the level of intelligence. The Mud Person becomes easily annoyed and short tempered at the stupidity of his family and friends. Afflicted Mud People learn to hide their new intelligence, but some become so desperate they commit suicide before the transformation is complete.

The transformation to Muck Ogre takes several years, during which time the unfortunate's body mass increases 600% to 1000%, most of which is fat. His or her skin turns brown or black, growing three centimeters thick and becoming as tough as armor. Raspy bristles of hair grow all over the body. The Muck Ogre winds up resembling a cross between a frog and a pig.

The worst part about the transformation is the cruelty of the normal Mud People. Those undergoing the Transformation are often penned up and ridiculed, objects of scorn. The attitude of the Muck Ogre deteriorates from caring about the safety of their young to concern with nothing more than their own survival. They become angry and dejected, eventually mirroring the cruelty of their previous families.

APPEARANCE OF THE MUD PEOPLE

The Mud People are tall and thin. Their hair and skin are lustrous bronze, and they have little body hair. The men never have facial hair. Their facial features are delicate and vulnerable. The women can be stunningly beautiful.

*TWO MUD PEOPLE SHUN
THEIR TRANSFORMING COUSIN*

SEA PEOPLE

Sea People are good natured, inquisitive, and intelligent. They value wisdom over all other traits and spend a good deal of their time accumulating wisdom from others.

The Sea People live in rivers, lakes, and oceans throughout Ringworld. They cannot survive in deserts, and detest bogs and swamps. They can live outside the water for brief periods and can actually run faster than a human on land for short distances. They have trouble adapting other hominid species' technologies to their environment and have learned not to be disappointed when equipment doesn't work satisfactorily.

The culture of the Sea People is based around extended families. They live in sprawling underwater lodges located in and around islands. They prefer their habitats unspoiled by other hominids and hide themselves well. The Sea People sometimes have conflicts with Muck Ogres, and have occasional contact with Ghouls (who have no claim to their dead).

APPEARANCE

The Sea People reach an average height of one and a half to two meters. Their bodies have the general proportions of otters: lithe bodies, small ears, and short legs. Their hands are partially webbed and the fingers taper into claws.

Sea Peoples' sense of smell and taste are extremely sharp. Unlike dolphins, their hearing is not well attuned to underwater functioning, an unusual development for an aquatic, hominid, species.

ONE OF THE SEA PEOPLE REACHES FOR THE SURFACE

VAMPIRES

The Vampires are one of the most beautiful and deadly species on Ringworld. They breathe pheromones, the hominid super-stimulus chemical that marks sexual readiness, from exocrine glands in the throat and upper respiratory tract; the pheromone is also excreted by their skin, transferred upon contact.

The pheromones send most hominids into a frenzy of sexual abandon. The urge is immediate and frantic, and victims would throw themselves out of buildings to be with the Vampire. Once the victim is in the Vampire's embrace, the creature pierces its prey's jugular and drinks the blood, occasionally eating certain organs and tissues to revitalize its pheromone-producing glands.

Fortunately, Vampires are uncommon. Every hominid culture despises them and wages genocidal wars whenever the creatures become too widespread. The City Builders are responsible for the distribution of Vampires across Ringworld, breeding the creatures for their pheromones, which are then distilled into vampire-scent used in rishathra. Some elderly and decadent City Builders maintain toothless Vampires for rishathra, a practice so loathsome that the creatures are kept secret. "Vampire lover" is one of the most vicious insults on Ringworld.

VAMPIRE HABITATS

Vampires live in temperate regions, taking shelter in caves or lightly wooded areas. They prefer to bathe before a hunt to avoid the sharp senses of species such as the Night People (who find Vampire pheromones to be a particularly unpleasant smell). Ruined cities are another favorite spot for these creatures, especially if there is a nearby lake or river.

A VAMPIRE IN HER LAIR

PSIONICS

162 INTRODUCTION TO PSIONICS
162 TELEPATHY
163 TELEKINESIS
164 FARSENSING

PSIONICS

The term "psionics" is a word of unknown origin used to describe the study of powers of the mind. First contact with the Thrint revealed that there is a broad range of psionic ability and potential to the races of Known Space. The Thrint were the greatest wielders of psionic energy, developing the Power which gave them influence over their slave races. Kzinti telepaths have the ability to read minds over great distances. Like the Slavers, the Grogs can also exert a psionic influence.

The current theory of psionics is that its "power" is not directed as a beam of energy from the mind of the wielder. It is instead a type of probability manipulation that originates from specific parts of the brain, affecting the *sequence space* of the universe. Sequence space is a mathematical model used to describe the range of possible events in a given hypothetical region, in this case the mind of the psionicist to the "target" area. Telepathy, which is known to originate in the right lobe of the human brain, has a sequence space "plane" in that part of the brain, with another at the target area, and a third leading to the rest of the universe. In the given range of probabilities, the "effect" of the psionic ability is telepathy. From a different part of the brain, the effect might be telekinesis.

The sequence space theory of psionics is similar to the idea of human psychic luck, which was theorized by the Puppeteers and brought to experiment with the Birthright Lotteries. Psychic luck is similar to psionic ability, except that two of its three planes of probability extend into the universe.

Possessing a clairvoyant ability is grounds for immediate entry to the ARM. Other abilities are definite bonuses for application, but they are not viewed with the same interest as clairvoyance.

TELEPATHY

Telepathy is the psionic field that gives the user the ability to enter into various mind-to-mind contact with living beings. A fair number of humans have a primitive form of telepathy that gives them "feelings" about other people. The Kzinti and Grogs have telepathy powerful enough to read the exact thoughts of a target.

Some common names and abilities used by telepathic specialists for their powers are:

Life Sense
Allows the user to detect other life forms in the immediate area.

Empathy
The ability to read and influence the emotions of others.

(Slaver) Mind Shield
An extremely rare power which defends the user against mental influence. This power was possessed by all Slavers.

Pure Telepathy
The ability to read the thoughts of another.

Plateau Eyes
This is an extremely limited psionic ability which makes the user "invisible" if the user can make eye contact with a target. The target immediately experiences a total loss of interest in the existence of the user and forgets the psionicist exists.

This power manifests itself ten times more often on Plateau than anywhere else in Known Space. A user unable to control the power or ignorant of its existence can become "lost" in society.

TELEKINESIS
Telekinesis is the talent which allows the psionicist to move objects without touching them. Powerful users of telekinetics have not been discovered outside of Slaver history.

Movement
Movement allows the user to move a number of kilograms of weight. Less powerful users can only move a few grams.

Invisible Arm
This is a strange and limited form of telekinesis that sometimes occurs with the loss of a limb. The psionicist "grows" an invisible arm (for instance) that replaces the one lost. The arm has the normal abilities of the original, including strength and tactile sensation. This is strange enough, but some invisible arms have been documented as penetrating stasis fields, allowing the user to feel the contents.

Bullet
Not a Thrint name, this power allows the user to hurl a projectile with the force of a gun.

Pyrokinesis

The use of this power causes combustible materials to ignite. The normal temperature generated by pyrokenesis is 120° Centigrade.

FARSENSING

Clairvoyance is the ability to perceive events over distance and, sometimes, time. This is a talent most often thought of as fortune telling.

Possessing a clairvoyant ability is grounds for immediate entry to the ARM.

Sense Danger

This is a "sixth sense" that gives the impression that "something isn't right." The greater the danger, the more pronounced the impression.

Clairvoyance

The actual ability to see events in other places. This power is rarely controllable in any but Kzinti telepaths.

Precognition

This talent seems to be an extension of sense danger, except that it gives pre-impression of any event. Like clairvoyance, this is a near-impossible talent to control.

CANDICE RAE DAVID

Known as C.R. to ARM, Candice is the only known human to possess psionic powers in all three fields of the science. Her greatest ability is Plateau Eyes, which she said she used when young to escape her parents and sneak off into the night.

EQUIPMENT OF KNOWN SPACE

166	STARSHIPS
166	SINCLAIR MONOFILAMENT CHAIN
166	DEEP-RADAR
168	MINIDOC™
168	MICROMIND™
168	TRACY
168	INERTIAL MAP
170	SIMWEB
170	STASIS FIELD GENERATOR
172	DROUD
172	TRANSPORT BOOTHS
172	LIFT BELT
172	VARIABLE SWORD
174	LASER WEAPONS
174	JINXIAN DUELING PISTOL
174	SLAVER DISINTEGRATOR
176	GAUSS WEAPONS
176	TASP
176	FRICTIONLESS ARMOR

STARSHIPS

Starships, of one type or another, are the only means of planetary travel. Not even the Puppeteers have been able to create stepping disks that work from system to system.

Starsails, Bussard ramscoops, and other, older, propulsion units have given way to fusion engines, reactionless thrusters, and gravity polarizers. Fusion engines use electromagnetic radiation and ions for propulsion. Reactionless thrusters use neutrinos to create their thrust; these were originally obtained from the Puppeteers. Gravity polarizers were used by the Kzinti in the Man-Kzin wars. They are energy inefficient, generating artifical gravity planes to pull a ship in the desired direction.

The only way to travel between the stars at non-relativistic speeds is with the Quantum I hyperdrive shunt, which unfortunately cause the instant destruction of ships when used in a gravity well. They are common throughout every region of space.

The most prized ships in Known Space are the General Products hulls. Made completely of a single complex molecule, the hulls are completely impervious to all forms of matter, though antimatter can still destroy them (this was never advertised). The GP hulls are transparent but are painted to avoid the insanity caused by the hyperspace blindspot. Many customers customize their GP hulls, adding wings, advanced weaponry, or engines.

Despite their amazing safety, the only drawback to General Product hulls is that their designs are incredibly boring. The GP 1 hull is a thirty centimeter sphere used for probes. The GP 2 hull is another sphere, but is ninety meters in diameter, the most common found in Human Space. The GP 3 hull are thirty-five meter diameter cylinders, one hundred and fifty meters long, with tapered ends and a flat underside for landings. The GP 4 hull is a sphere three hundred meters in diameter mostly used by the few governments who can afford them for colony ships. The GP 4 is also the only hull that can house the Quantum II hyperdrive shunt.

SINCLAIR MONOFILAMENT CHAIN

Sinclair monofilament chain is used to tow the most tremendous loads. The chain is a complex, artificially-reinforced single molecule that can cut normal matter with a tug. Each strand is less than a micron thick.

Sinclair chain cannot cut General Products hull material, scrith, or other chain, though it can eventually cut through hullmetal. Monofilament chain dispensers are usually hullmetal spools with hullmetal bobs at the ends so the chain can be played out to the appropriate length.

DEEP-RADAR

Deep-radar uses low power hyperwave pulses induced by neutrino emission to provide near-instantaneous information about objects within range of the radar's beam. Normal matter appears as a translucent image on the tri-dee screen with all but the most dense substances shown in detail, such as the collapsed matter of a neutron star. The deep-radar image of a G-type sun would appear as a gray disk darkening to black at the center. Stasis fields, which reflect all neutrinos, appear as flecks of pure black; it is easy to hunt for Slaver stasis boxes with deep-radar.

There is no Doppler effect with deep-radar. An object's velocity can be determined by plotting the intervals of successive hyperwave pulses.

SINCLAIR MONOFILAMENT CHAIN

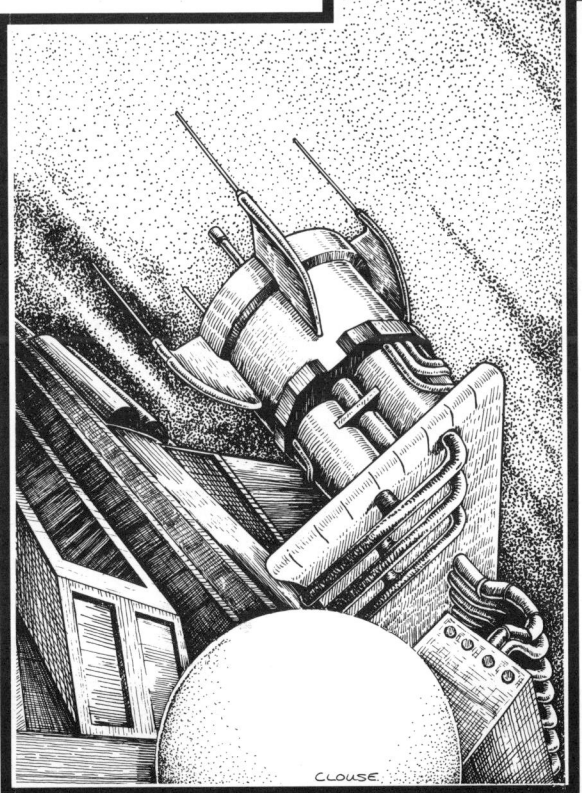

DEEP RADAR

PORTABLE DEEP RADAR

Equipment of Known Space *The Guide to Larry Niven's Ringworld*

A deep-radar set can be focused to examine an object with greater detail. The interior of some dense objects, or very small or light objects can sometimes be seen, but the detail is not sufficient for most needs. Other sensors are typically used for greater detail when the deep-radar finds something of interest.

MINIDOCS™

MiniDocs™ are portable medical kits which can automatically administer aid to a patient. Wounds can be healed, broken limbs set, and antibiotics or other drugs applied to an ailing explorer. As long as the unit has energy and a fresh supply of bandages, it attempts to heal the patient.

The MiniDoc™ has three folded arms with dexterous fingers, each ending in a specific medical tool such as a laser scalpel or clean-field projector. The kit can perform any operation from removing an appendix to extracting a bullet, but cannot perform organ transplants or other specialized tasks.

The unit is always set in one of two modes. The first is inferential, where the MiniDoc™ acts on its own volition, analyzing the patient and performing what it thinks are the necessary steps to preserve the patient's life. The second mode is deferential; the unit performs no actions without the commands of the user.

The MiniDoc™ begins its task by scanning the patient for one minute before beginning treatment. This scan is bypassed if the subject is in critical condition. This often leads to the MiniDoc™ failing to diagnose a secondary problem, which is definitely bad for the patient. This has led to the phrase, "as untrustworthy as a MiniDoc™."

MICROMIND™

The MicroMind™ is the size of a hand calculator, accepting pen-based and one-handed keyboard input as well as minimal voice commands. The computer is capable of performing many sophisticated tasks at once, employing banks of stacked very large scale integrated chips (SVLSIC) and planar memory pack (PMP) modules for multitasking and multi-processing. MicroMinds™ can easily communicate with larger computers, accepting and transferring data through short range infra-red transmission or direct access universal cables.

There are numerous InfoTabs available for the MicroMind™, providing the user with a wealth of information. Alien language translators, full length histories, and technical specifications are just a few of the most popular InfoTabs.

TRACY

Tracy is the general term for any wrist-worn tri-dee transceiver worn by explorers, security guards, and people on recreational cruises in wild territory. Its range is extremely limited unless boosted by a base station, which makes it useful for police and forest rangers who patrol a limited area.

Tracys give the wearer a limited holographic and audio display. The fidelity of the images is fairly low, even on the top-end models. The unit's range is about two kilometers, but the signal is sometimes blocked by tension wires and metal buildings.

INERTIAL MAP

The inertial map is a relatively simple device that uses motion sensors, compasses, and similar equipment to cross reference the user's direction with a pre-plotted electronic map. The user's

MicroMind™

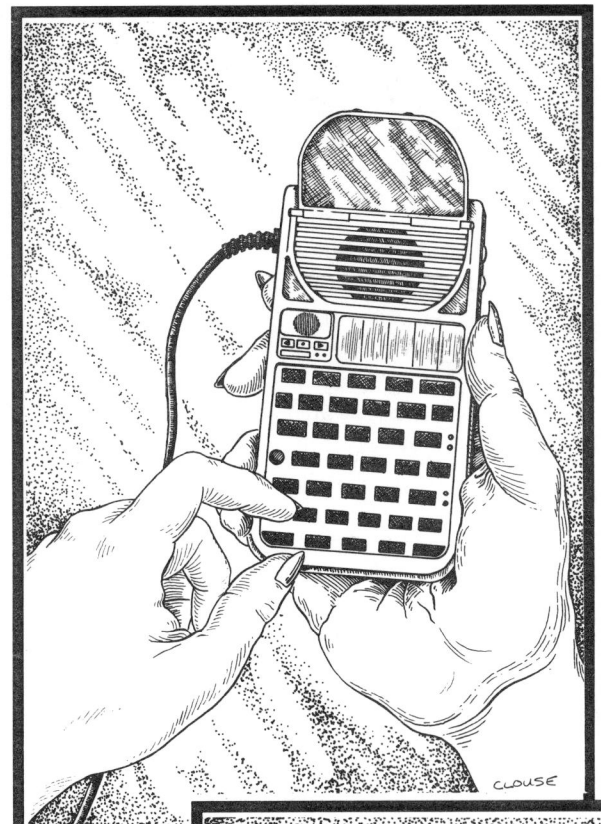

INERTIAL MAP LOCATOR

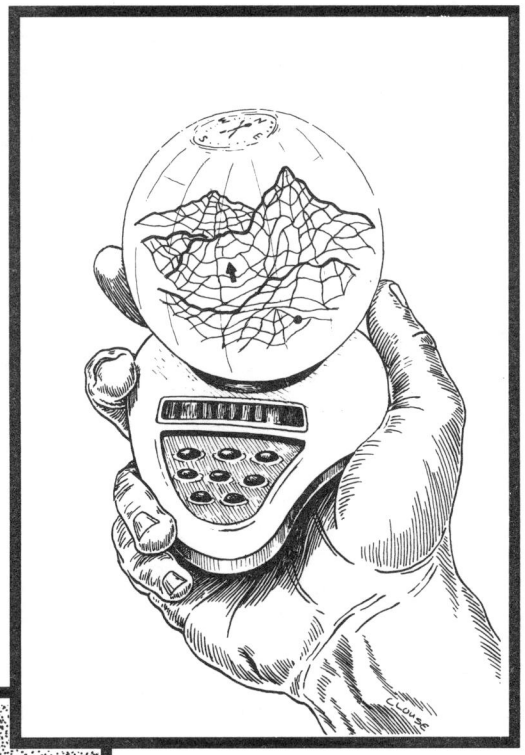

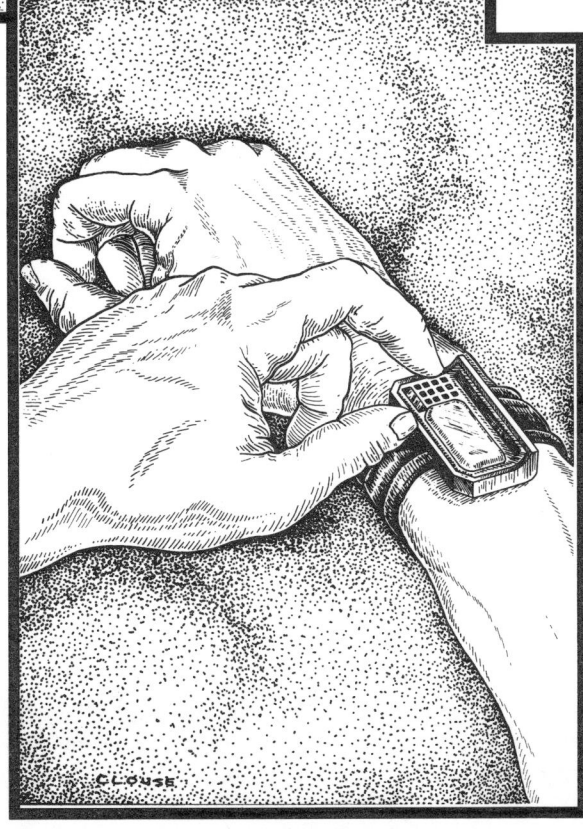

TRACY

Equipment of Known Space — The Guide to Larry Niven's Ringworld

location from his original position is constantly registered on the holo-screen in terms of arrows and topographic information.

The inertial map is usually hand-held. Units of the ARM have inertial maps built into their protective helmets.

SIMWEB

Simwebs allow Known Space explorers to garner experience before encountering danger. The simweb creates a virtual reality for the user, employing anesthetic drugs and neural stimulation rather than primitive "screen helmets," which only provided visual information. This new reality is so genuine that simweb users are able to learn, in a very real sense, how to climb cliffs, move safely in spacewalks, and anything else that can be found in a simweb's program banks.

Simwebs look like cocoons made from fibrous plastics and other resilient materials. They are built for many Known Space species, including humans, dolphins, Kzinti, and Kdatlyno. Only one simweb was ever sold to the Puppeteers. The cocoons provide food and water for the duration of the "adventure," which can sometimes take several days for the user to gain the full advantage of experience.

There are two drawbacks to using the simweb. The first is simulated death, which can occur during an adventure either through a mistake by a user (such as not spiking his rope to the cliff face) or by "normal" events, which can be anything from a rockslide to the attack of a tiger, depending on the scenario. Simweb death incurs a period of depression on the user, which can last as long as a month.

The other drawback to simwebs occur when explorers die too often in adventures; they sometimes tend to lose their sense of place in the real world and blur the lines between simweb scenario and reality. On occasion, this can turn into simweb addiction, which is just as potent as droud addiction.

If a simweb session needs to be ended in an emergency, the simweb computer creates a suitable transition for the explorer and the session ends within an hour. SRS, or Simweb Release Shock, has caused at least ten known deaths since the simweb was created.

STASIS FIELD GENERATORS

Stasis fields create bubbles of energy where time moves at a slower rate. There are nine quantum levels of fields, where the lowest translates a one minute to six hour ratio, and the highest (used exclusively by the Tnuctipun) a one minute to 1.5 billion year ratio. All conditions are maintained within the field, including charges and spin on unstable atoms.

Anything put into stasis must have a conductive surface; a special conductive coating can be applied to the object. The field forms one minute after the power has been activated. There is no known method to stop the formation of a stasis field once the sequence has been initiated.

A stasis field thrown over the first temporarily nullifies the first field. The contents of a stasis field can sometimes be photographed when the fields are "flickered" from the first to the second without actually harming the contents.

The fields can be controlled by using an atomic clock to switch off the field at a preset time. It is also possible to mount a switch which projects through the field. When the switch is thrown, a tiny stasis generator throws another field over the first, sending an "off" signal to

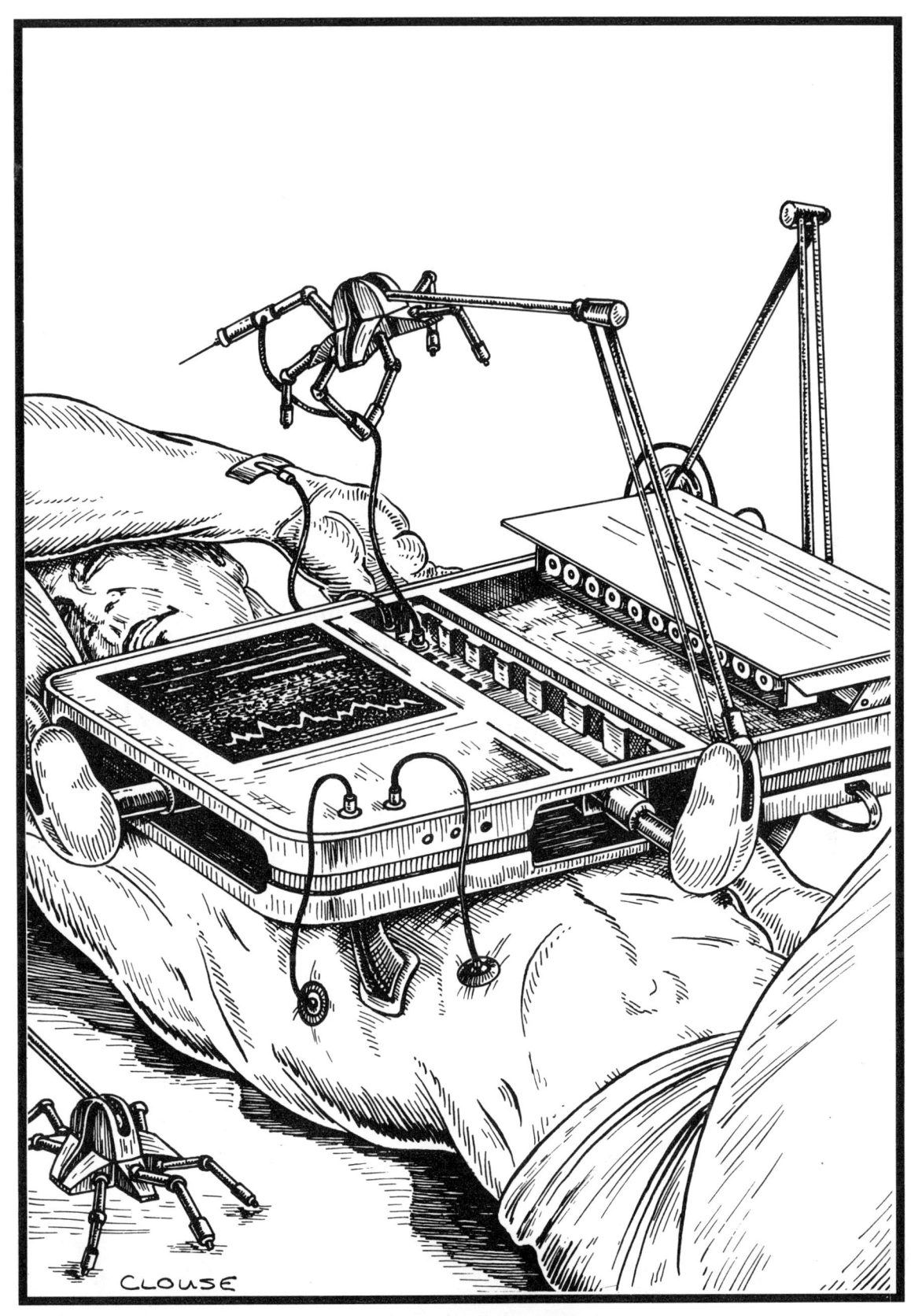

MiniDoc™

Equipment of Known Space — *The Guide to Larry Niven's Ringworld*

the power source. External power sources provide the simplest disablement method, as they can be simply turned off.

Psionic abilities directly related to the powers of cognition do not work through a stasis field. Abilities that employ the use of "luck" or empathy occasionally work through a field. Exotic powers such as an "imaginary limb" are known to work through fields, but these psionic users are even more rare than Slaver stasis boxes.

DROUD

A droud is the greatest threat to mankind. Its wires connect directly to the pleasure centers of the brain, where a small trickle of current keeps the "wirehead" in ecstasy as long as there is power. The experience is so pure and joyful that the user is addicted within days and dies within weeks from starvation and dehydration.

Most Known Space governments do not interfere in the personal lives of their citizens, so drouds are not always illegal. However, wireheads are often held in pity or contempt when their secret is discovered.

TRANSPORT BOOTHS

Transport booths are the reason that Earth's once illustrious cities have lost their personality, at least according to certain aged explorers. Booths allow the instantaneous transfer of matter between points and are primarily used by people to get from one city to the next. This has made metropolitan areas more homogenous because travelers can easily share their cultures with other parts of the world.

The maximum range of a single transfer booth is about two hundred kilometers. Booths will not transmit until the door is secured, a destination selected, and money paid. A booth can transfer up to twenty tons, but most are only used for transporting people and are sized accordingly.

Wunderland, Plateau, and Jinx also have transport booth networks across their surfaces. Other planets have short range booth arrangements, but long distance travel is still done through air and ground vehicles.

LIFT BELT

Lift belts cannot normally be used in Earth cities; all flying traffic is strictly regulated and manual piloting is illegal. Lift belts are more commonly used on other worlds.

A lift belt is little more than a MAGLEV generator shoved inside a comfortable housing, with controls for attitude and speed controlled by handgrips. They are easy to use and sturdy.

VARIABLE SWORD

Variable swords are popular with Kzinti. The swords are lightweight handles containing small stasis field generators and a spool of monofilament chain. The chain can be extended to a range of thirty meters; a small red marker-ball is fitted to the end of the chain to mark position. The sword's exceptional range can make it dangerous to friends as well as enemies.

Sinclair monofilament chain cannot cut through stasis fields, scrith, or General Products hulls. It can eventually cut through hullmetal, but the user has to do a lot of sawing.

The variable knife is similar to the

VARIABLE KNIFE

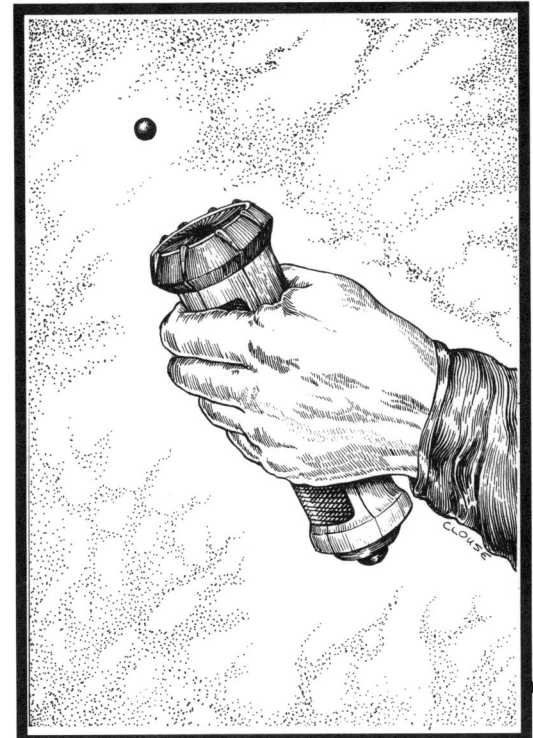

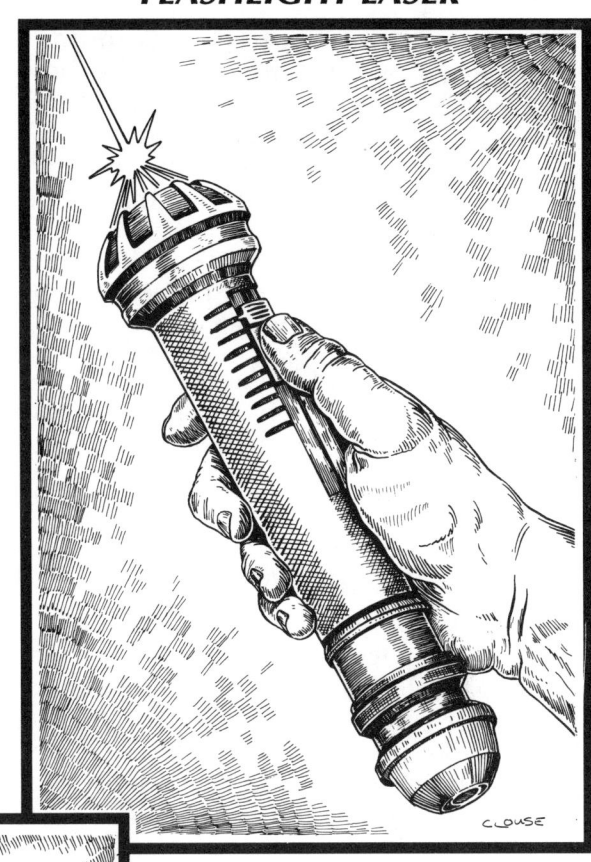

FLASHLIGHT LASER

VARIABLE SWORD

Equipment of Known Space

The Guide to Larry Niven's Ringworld

variable sword, but has a maximum extension of only a few feet. Like the sword, there is a miniature stasis field generator that keeps the length of Sinclair monofilament chain taut, and there is a small red ball that marks the end of the chain. Sinclair chain cannot cut scrith, GP hulls, or stasis fields, and has difficulty cutting hullmetal, but does wonders against softer targets.

The stasis field generator has a maximum life of fifty-three years. For safety, a microcharge melts the generator.

LASER WEAPONS

Lasers are common weapons in Known Space, and like all deadly weapons, are illegal. They are reasonably efficient, powerful, and easy to maintain. The major drawbacks to lasers is that they are easily deflected by reflective surfaces and easy to defend against with clothes the same color as the beam. Their beams are also scattered by dust and clouds, though their frequencies may be tuned to ignore such detrimental atmospheric conditions.

The two most common laser weapons are the hand beamer and the laser pistol. Neither are particularly noteworthy, except that the beamer's small size make it the perfect weapon for concealment and skull-duggery, while the laser pistol is commonly used by the ARM.

The flashlight laser is a multi-purpose tool, created by General Products. Its green beam can be used as a normal flashlight, or focused into one of the most deadly weapons in Known Space. The flashlight laser is created for attacking large numbers of targets, similar to attacking with a variable sword. The weapon is swung in a wide arc and can affect as many opponents as can be struck. The longer the beam stays on the target, the more damage the target takes.

The flashlight laser has ten focus settings. The first setting creates a beam three meters wide at twenty meters. The tenth setting, the most powerful, creates a beam .01 millimeters wide at twenty meters which can cut through five centimeters of steel in about a minute.

JINXIAN DUELING PISTOL

The Jinxian Dueling Pistol is one of the most elegantly designed weapons in Known Space. Like all stunners, it fires a subsonic beam that causes instant unconsciousness in opponents. The weapon uses energy according to the size of the target, which is set before firing. Stunners are also affected by range and the density of the atmosphere.

Despite their non-lethality, ownership of a Dueling Pistol is illegal. Penalties range from fines to short term imprisonment.

SLAVER DISINTEGRATOR

The Slaver disintegrator sub-atomically disassembles its target by suppressing the electron charge of its atoms from negative to neutral. The charge quickly restablishes itself, but the target has already fallen to molecular dust.

The beam continues to disintegrate as long as the trigger is pulled. It can cut through a cubic meter of stone in thirty seconds. The Slaver disintegrator has no effect on General Products hulls or scrith. Sinclair monofilament chain and hullmetal are easily destroyed by the disintegrator.

The Puppeteer disintegrator works on the same principles as the Slaver model, except that it has an additional emitter that suppresses the charge on the positron. Firing both barrels at a

LASER PISTOL

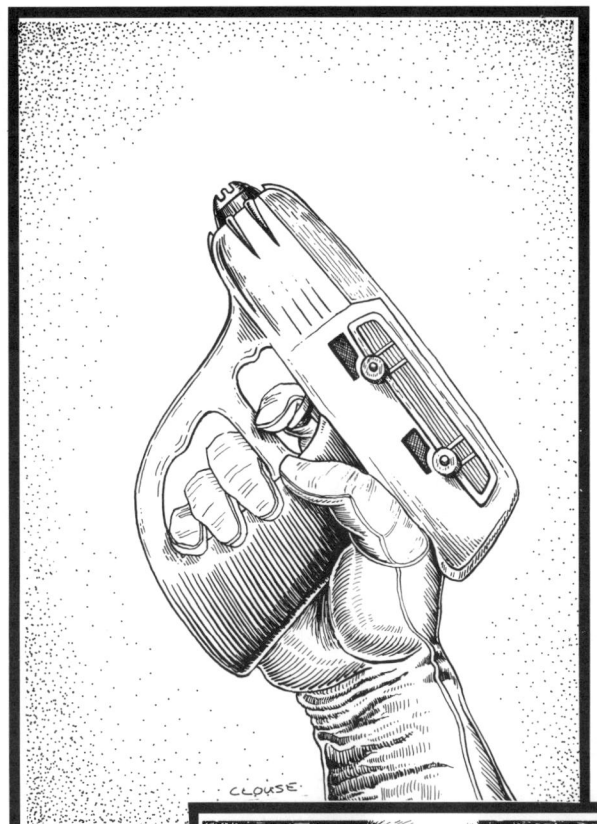

JINXIAN DUELING PISTOL

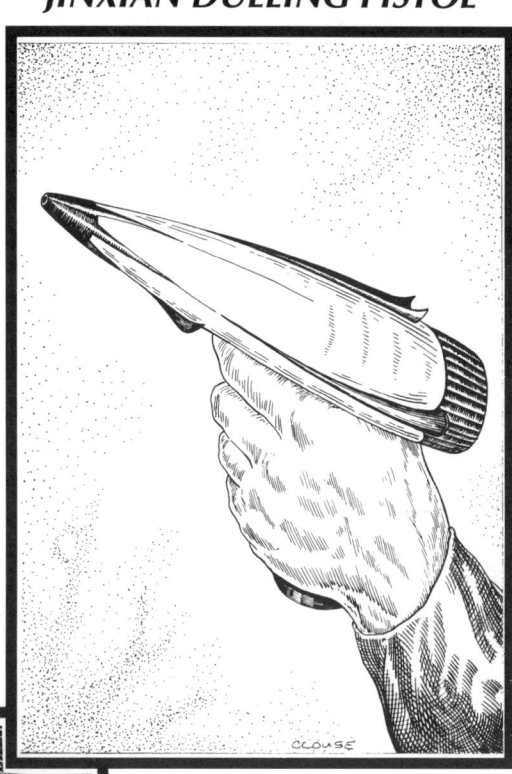

SLAVER DISINTEGRATOR

Equipment of Known Space — The Guide to Larry Niven's Ringworld

target creates a small atomic explosion.

Despite its additional power, the Puppeteer disintegrator cannot effect scrith or General Products hulls.

GAUSS WEAPONS

Gauss weapons use a magnetic linear accelerator to propel solid shot or explosive rounds. The rifle's clip holds twenty hypervelocity shells, while the pistol holds five; each shell is equipped with its own battery to activate the accelerator.

The gauss rifle is one of the heaviest weapons in Known Space, and is actually not often seen. It has a low rate of fire which makes it more useful for support work rather than personal combat. The weapon is so effective that light tanks are viable targets. The pistol is sometimes carried by top ARM agents.

Gauss weapons can be found in the coveted arsenals of some City Builder floating castles.

TASP

Tasps are illegal in Human Space. They stimulate the pleasure centers of the brain, much like a droud, causing the victim to stand around, oblivious and drunk with pleasure. They can sometimes cause "wire-addiction."

Human-built tasps are rifle-sized and suggestively shaped. They only effect humans and similar hominids. The Puppeteer tasps are small enough to be surgically implanted in their heads and can effect all species that have pleasure centers.

FRICTIONLESS ARMOR

Frictionless armor was originally developed by the Belters to protect them against dust and gravel storms. Frictionless surfaces are also very effective for deflecting bullets and other projectiles unless struck perpendicular to the surface.

The major drawbacks to frictionless armor is the loss of motion due to its bulk and the embarrassing comedic effect of falling and not being able to get back up.

ANDREW LEKER

Andrew is known as one of the most amazing minds in Known Space. A doctor of physics, mathematics, and philosophy, Andrew is also a computer scientist. He was the first to discover the axioms governing the behavior of artificial intelligences. This axiom was a critical factor in the creation of the MicroMind™ and many other common pieces of Known Space equipment.

GAUSS PISTOL

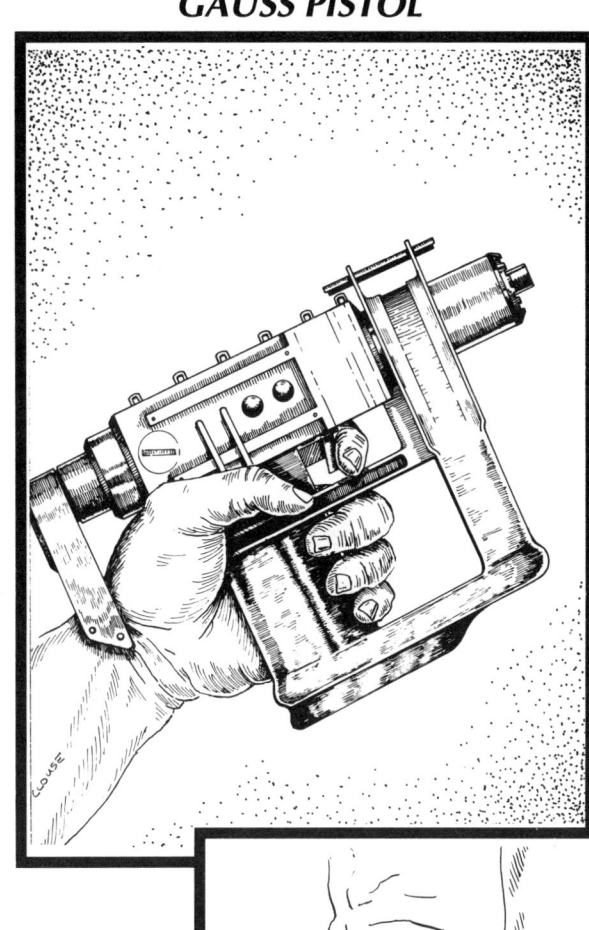

GAUSS RIFLE

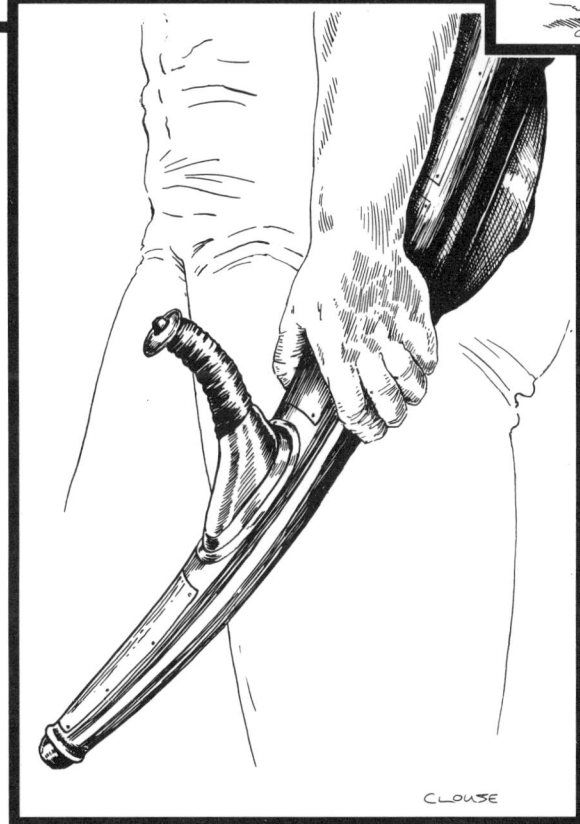

TASP

Equipment of Known Space   *The Guide to Larry Niven's Ringworld*

LIFT BELT

TRANSPORT BOOTH

FLYCYCLE

The Guide to Larry Niven's Ringworld — Equipment of Known Space

VAC SUIT

FRICTIONLESS ARMOR

SEA SUIT

Equipment of Known Space — The Guide to Larry Niven's Ringworld

SIMWEB

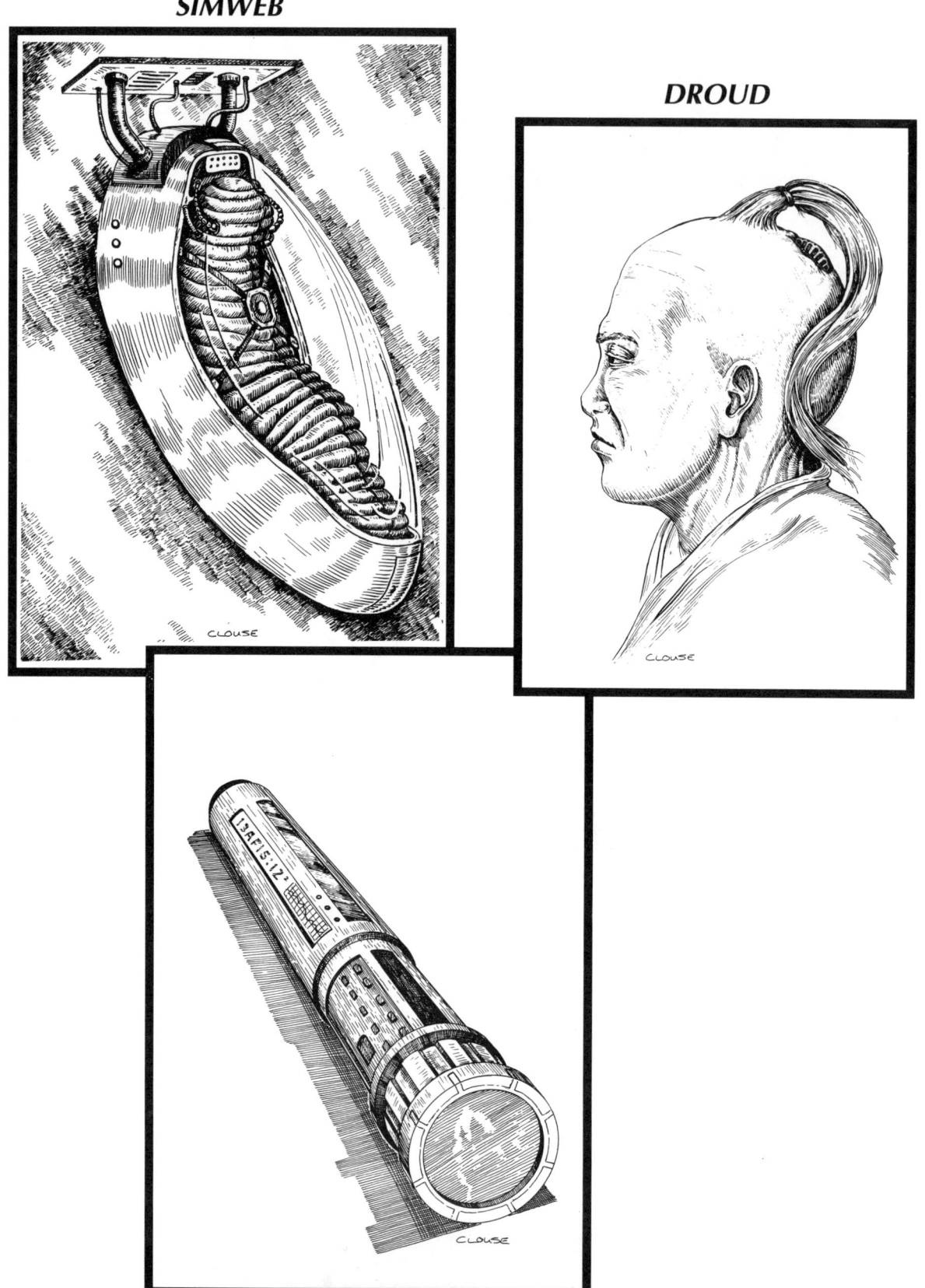

DROUD

SENSOR DISK

The Guide to Larry Niven's Ringworld　　　　　　　　　　Equipment of Known Space

STARSHIP STASIS FIELD GENERATOR

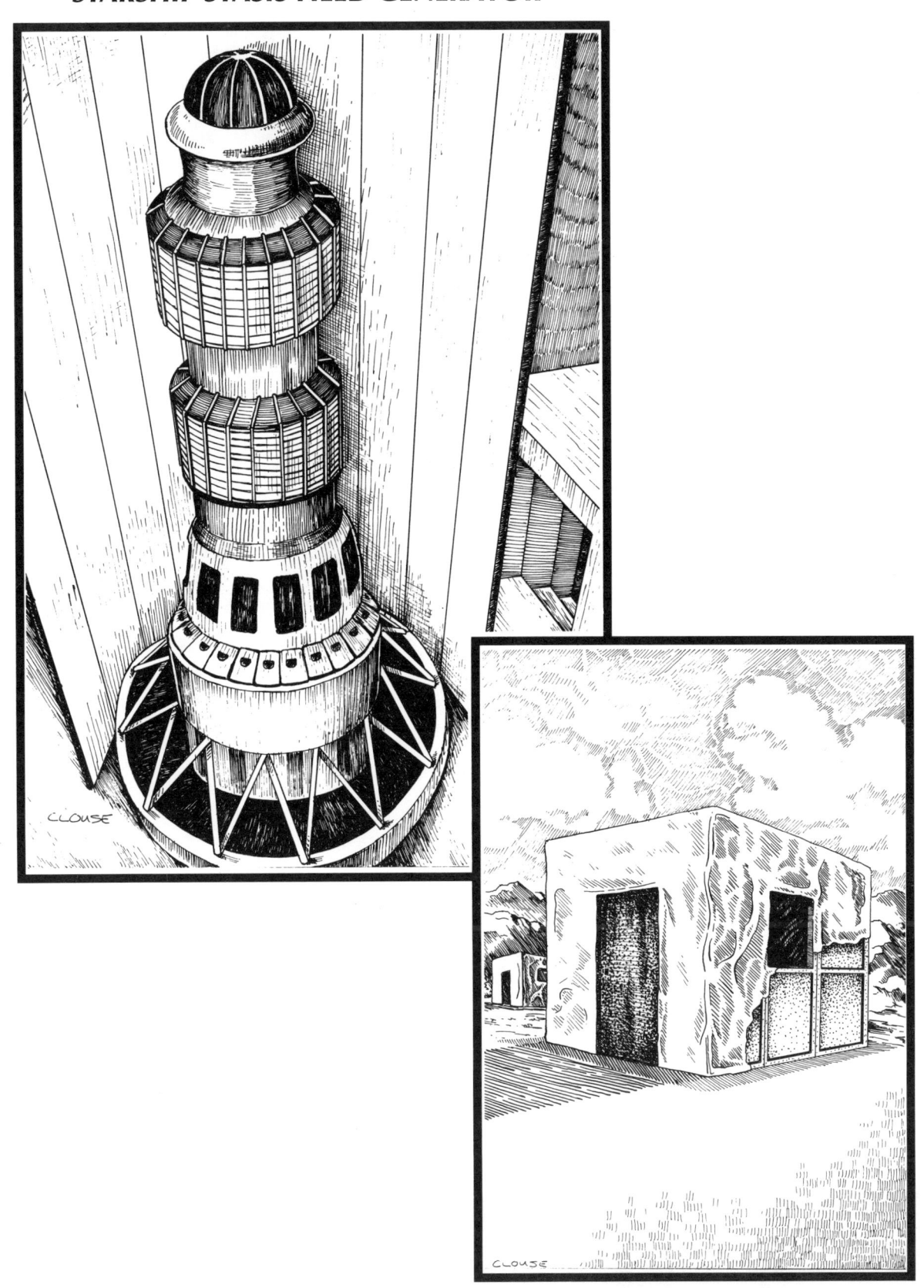

SHELTER BLOCK

Equipment of Known Space

The Guide to Larry Niven's Ringworld

GLOSSARY

ALIEN
Any and all intelligent non-hominids.

ANTISPINWARD
The direction opposite to Ringworld's direction of spin. One of the four primary directions on Ringworld as defined by its rotation.

ARM
The United Nations special police force involved in monitoring alien-human affairs and high-technology.

ATTITUDE JETS
Bussard ramjets mounted on the outer rim walls to keep Ringworld stable in the plane of its orbit. Also small reaction motors for adjusting a spacecraft's orientation.

AUTODOC
Within their capability, these medical devices automatically diagnose and treat injury and illness. The best autodocs can handle almost every problem; less sophisticated units may deal only with superficial cuts, bruises, and hangovers. Autodocs are species specific; a human autodoc is of no use to a Kzin, for example.

BANDERSNATCHI
A huge, sentient slug-like creature created long ago by the Tnuctipun, originally engineered as food animals but were secretly given intelligence to spy on the Slavers.

BELT
The asteroid belt of Sol System.

BELTER
A citizen of the Belt.

BIRTHRIGHT LOTTERIES
Puppeteer manipulated experiment in human engineering that set up lotteries for the right to breed. The random drawing guaranteed a flatlander the right to be a parent regardless of the state of his or her genes or social conduct. Only the luckiest flatlanders could breed, selecting generations and generations of luckier and luckier humans–or so the Puppeteers thought.

BLIND SPOT
A disturbing perceptual phenomenon experienced during hyperspace flight. Prolonged viewing may cause insanity in humans.

BOOSTERSPICE
A drug neutralizing the aging process in humans. Most users maintain the apparent age they had when they began boosterspice treatment. A single dose lasts about 25 years. Boosterspice became available around 2425, synthesized from a native ragweed on Jinx. Originally, boosterspice was rare and fantastically expensive–only a handful of humans could afford treatment.

BREEDERS
The second stage in the life cycle of Pak and other hominid species. Human beings normally spend their adult lives arrested in this phase of development since tree-of-life root, the biological agent which triggers third-stage growth, is unavailable.

BUSSARD, R.W
Pre-fusion era physicist who originated the theory of the interstellar ramjet.

CANYON
A former Kzinti world annexed by humanity at the end of the third Man-Kzin war. Its one habitable region is a long, deep canyon gouged by the Wunderland Treatymaker.

CETACEAN
General term for Dolphins, Sperm Whales, and Orcas; the order of marine animals to which those species belong.

CETACEAN RIGHTS ACT
Passed in 2017, this act granted full human rights to all sentient cetaceans.

CHMEE
Kzinti ambassador to humanity who earned his full name as a member of the first Ringworld expedition (formerly Speaker-to-Animals). Chmee was kidnapped for the second expedition.

CITY BUILDER
A member of the sophisticated hominid species who built Ringworld's floating cities and who traveled to the stars.

COMDISC
Compact, hand carried, disk-shaped communicator often linked to a ship's computer.

COM-LASER
Any laser communication beam or device; standard shipboard equipment.

CRASHLANDER
A native of the planet We Made It.

CZILTANG-BRONE
A device which appears to be a scrith osmosis-generator.

DEEP RADAR
Pulsed-neutrino system for viewing the internal structure of material objects; strongly reflected by stasis fields and collapsed matter.

DOLPHINS
Sentient cetacean species native to Earth. Dolphins have colonized the oceans of several human worlds.

DOWN
Formerly a Kzinti world and home world of the Grogs.

DROUD
A small device that plugs into the skull of a current addict. It meters the electrical flow to the pleasure center of the addict's brain.

EYESTORM
A major storm on Ringworld, resembling a vertical, rolling hurricane, usually created by a meteor puncture through the Ringworld floor.

FALAN
A Ringworld unit of time. A falan is 75 Ringworld days long, equalling ten turns of the Ringworld. Equivalent to 3 months UNS time.

FALL OF CITIES
The disaster which ended the City Builder civilization. Caused by the Puppeteer-induced superconductor plague, its name refers to its most dramatic manifestation, the fall and destruction of most of the floating cities.

THE FAR LOOK
A hypnotic condition experienced by sentient beings who continually

Glossary of Ringworld Terms　　　　　　　*The Guide to Larry Niven's Ringworld* stare into the depths of outer space from space ships.

FERTILITY BOARD
A subsection of the United Nations which makes and enforces birth control laws.

FIST-OF-GOD
An enormous mountain located spinward of the Great Oval Ocean created by a massive meteor strike that blasted upward through the Ringworld floor.

FLASHLIGHT LASER
A powerful, adjustable-beam handheld laser.

FLATLANDER
A human from Earth, usually one that has never been in space.

FLEET-OF-WORLDS
The five Puppeteer planets journeying toward the Magellanic Clouds to escape the radiation created by the galactic core explosion.

FLUP
The water-logged soil which dredges scrape from the bottom of Ringworld oceans. Flup is recycled through a system of processing tubes to the surface where it is redeposited into the ecosystem via the Spill Mountains.

FLYCYCLE
A one-seated flying vehicle designed by the General Products Corporation.

FUSION
The process by which the nuclei of light elements (usually isotopes of hydrogen) unite to form heavier nuclei, releasing tremendous amounts of energy.

GALACTIC CORE
The dense, star-cloud at the center of most galaxies. In the Milky Way galaxy, the cloud is 7000 light years across and its nucleus is nearly 30,000 light years from Known Space. The Milky Way's core was discovered by the Puppeteers to be undergoing a cataclysmic explosion sending waves of deadly radiation that will engulf Known Space in 20,000 years.

GREAT OCEANS
The two vast salt oceans located on opposite sides of Ringworld. They are so huge that each contains numerous 1:1 maps of entire planets dotted across its surface as isolated islands.

GENERAL PRODUCTS
A large Puppeteer-owned company that once dominated interstellar trade in Known Space and beyond. This commercial empire collapsed when nearly the entire race of Puppeteers left Known Space.

GENERAL PRODUCTS HULLS
These unique spacecraft hulls are the ultimate in safety, and are guaranteed impervious to normal matter in any form. Most are transparent only to visible light. GP hulls come in four basic types and are further customized by the user.

GRAVITY POLARIZER
A sub-light space drive widely used by Kzinti before the advent of thrusters; still found in older Known Space spacecraft.

GRAVITY WELL
A local distortion of space-time due to the presence of any massive object, such as a star or planet. See also Singularity.

GROGS
An intelligent alien race native to Down, in human space. Grogs are telepathic -able to influence the minds and control the bodies of most animals, aliens and humans. Fortunately, they are friendly.

HERO'S TONGUE
The native language of Kzin. To most humans the speech sounds like a rapidly spit-out string of insults, replete with screams, snarls, growls, and atonal inflections. Quieter expressions range from sharp, barely-audible single syllables to low, muted, furry rumblings.

HINDMOST
A Puppeteer ruler; also, the Puppeteer term for the leader of any group.

HOME
An Earthlike human colony world. In the 24th century, the inhabitants were mysteriously wiped out by an unknown phenomenon. It has since been repopulated

HOMINID
All creatures directly or indirectly evolved from Pak breeders. Humans are hominid, as are most Ringworld natives.

HORIZON HYPNOSIS
On Ringworld the infinity-horizon seems to go on forever and even the least suggestible human mind sometimes falls victim to this hypnotic trance while traveling for long periods over the surface.

HOT NEEDLE OF INQUIRY
The spacecraft used by the second Ringworld expedition; also, a Kzinti instrument of torture.

HUMAN SPACE
That volume of space occupied by stars with major human colony worlds; a portion of Known Space about 40 light years across.

HYPERDRIVE
The propulsion system used extensively by Known Space species to cross interstellar distances faster than the speed of light. The most accessible hyperdrive rate is three days to the light year (Quantum I).

HYPERWAVE
A nearly-instantaneous form of communication which works over interstellar distances but only outside the gravity-wells of suns.

IMPACT ARMOR
Flexible, leathery, personal armor which stiffens upon strong impact and distributes the blow equally to all portions of the armor. It is commonly worn as clothing in risky environments. it does not protect against beam weapons, radiation, poisonous gas, or other forms of attack.

INERTIALESS DRIVE
An extremely sophisticated version of the reactionless drive, which limits the buildup of relativistic mass during acceleration; used by the Outsiders and the Puppeteers.

INFINITY-HORIZON
On Ringworld there is no line where land curves

away from sky. Instead, land and sky merge into a uniform, hypnotic, horizontal band, where all colors blend gradually into the blue of sky.

It is a "vanishing plane" made up of an infinite number of vanishing points in every horizontal direction. Staring at this vanishing point can drive sentient beings insane.

INSTITUTE OF KNOWLEDGE
The major research lab and think tank in Known Space.

The institute was founded originally to study the gigantic slug-like Bandersnatchi, first encountered by colonists along the inhospitable shorelines of Jinx. Communication with Bandersnatchi has led to the study of Tnuctipun language and technology. Slaver stasis boxes have been nearly exclusive Institute provinces of study. The Institute has played a crucial role in understanding, displaying, and popularizing alien arts, science, and ways.

INTERWORLD
Originally a rudimentary tongue for human convenience in times of military emergency, the Interworld language grew steadily in sophistication, finally becoming the accepted interspecies language used throughout Known Space.

JINX
One of the oldest, most populous human colony worlds.

KDAPTIST
Heretical Kzinti religious cult that believes God made mankind in his image, not Kzinti.

KDATLYNO [k'DAT-lie-no]
Once the slaves of the Kzinti, this race of massive nightmarish-looking aliens are blind to visible light but have sensitive acoustic-sonar. They are well known for their touch-sculptures, an exotic art form valued throughout Known Space.

KNOWN SPACE
That volume of interstellar space explored by humanity or by humanity's alien neighbors. Known Space is about 80 light years in diameter. Human Space is a portion of Known Space.

KZINTI [k'ZIN-tee]
Large cat-like alien carnivores who dream of conquering the universe. Their interstellar empire once nearly engulfed Known Space.

LANDER
General name for a ground-to-orbit craft designed to land on the surface of a planet. Most landers are not equipped with hyperdrive.

LONGEVITY DRUG
A rare substance made from tree-of-life root found on Ringworld. It is of great value on the Ringworld.

LONG SHOT
The first Quantum II hyperdrive starship, piloted by Beowulf Shaeffer to the galactic core, and by Louis Wu to the Puppeteer Fleet-of-Worlds.

LYING BASTARD
The spacecraft used by the first Ringworld expedition.

MAGLEV
Magnetic Levitation.

MAGELLANIC CLOUDS
The major satellite galaxies of the Milky Way. The destination of the Puppeteer Fleet-of-Worlds.

MAN-KZIN WARS
A series of interstellar conflicts, including four wars and many major incidents, spanning 300 years from the mid-24th to the mid-27th centuries. With the help of Puppeteer intervention, all wars were won by humans.

MASS INDICATOR
In hyperspace flight, a device for detecting singularities. Also mass sensor, mass-pointer.

MAP ROOM
Holographic projection room in which detailed images of the Ringworld's surface may be viewed via old tapes or live telescopic camera mounted on the shadow squares.

MEMORY BUBBLE
Information storage units used by Known Space computers.

METEOR DEFENSE SYSTEM
Solar flare-powered gas laser controlled from the shadow squares, capable of vaporizing any object that might impact the surface of Ringworld.

NEREID
Neptune's smaller moon; the site of the Outsider base in Sol system.

NESSUS
The mad Puppeteer who led the first expedition to Ringworld, in 2850, enticed by the Experimentalist Hindmost for the right to breed.

NEUTRINO
Elusive, nearly-massless sub-atomic particle that travels just below lightspeed, to which normal matter is transparent.

NEUTRONIUM
Collapsed matter having the density of a neutron star.

NORMAL SPACE
Space-time continuum described by Einsteinian relativity, the physical laws of which all sub-light spacecraft must obey.

OFFWORLDER
A person not native to the world where he or she is currently. Pejoratively used, especially by flatlanders.

ORCA
Largest of the sentient species of Dolphins; native to Earth.

ORGAN BANK
Repository of human (or alien) organs and limbs for purposes of transplant.

OUTSIDERS
An advanced alien race from beyond Known Space, Outsiders are fragile beings adapted to life in the cold interstellar void. Outsiders travel from the galactic core to the tips of the spiral arms at sub-light speeds, often following starseeds. They trade in information and technology.

PAK
A race of warlike, xenophobic hominids native to an Earthlike world in the galactic core. Their lifecycle has three stages: childhood, breeder, and protector (the

Glossary of Ringworld Terms — *The Guide to Larry Niven's Ringworld*

protector stage is initiated by eating a virus contained in tree-of-life root). All Ringworld hominids as well as humanity evolved from Pak breeders.

PATRIARCHY
The Kzin government; also, the Kzinti families with highest status, equivalent to royalty, whose names bear the -Rift suffix.

PHEROMONE
Super-powerful hormonal biochemicals that stimulate species-specific physiological or behavioral responses.

PHSSTHPOK
The only Pak protector encountered by humans, it was attempting to rescue what it thought were Pak breeders stranded on Earth. Instead it found a race of highly advanced and mutated humans which it immediately signaled for termination.

PLASMA
Super-heated, ionized gas such as that in a solar flare or fusion reactor.

PLATEAU
Major human colony world in the Tau Ceti system. Its habitable surface area is limited to the upper slopes of an immense mountain, Mt. Lookitthat, which forms a maze of plateaus above the planet's hot, dense lower atmosphere.

PLATEAU EYES
A limited psionic ability found in some natives of Plateau giving them strange hypnotic powers.

PLATEAU TRANCE
A hallucinatory trance state of autohypnosis induced by long looks down into the swirling void mists off the edges of Plateau. A group of religious clairvoyants living on Plateau trace visions of Mist Demons contacted through Plateau Trance. They claim the demons live in the poisonous lower depths of the planet's surface.

PORT
To the left as one faces spinward on the surface of Ringworld.

PROTECTOR
The third stage in the lifecycle of the Pak, triggered by eating tree-of-life root. A virus in the root causes a metamorphosis turning the hominid into a very strong and cunning, armored warrior with the one overriding motivation to protect the lives of their bloodline descendants.

PSIONICS
The science of direct mind/machine interface; also, certain mental powers controlled by the mechanisms in the right parietal lobe of the brain–inaccessible to the conscious minds of most humans.

PUPPETEERS
An advanced alien species of two-headed, tripedal herbivores that once dominated interstellar trade in Known Space and beyond. In the Ringworld era, nearly all Puppeteers have embarked on an exodus from Known Space, fleeing the radiation front of the galactic core explosion.

QUANTUM I HYPERDRIVE
Commonly used in Known Space during the Ringworld era, the Quantum I travels at the first quantum rate of hyperspace travel, three UNS days to the light year.

QUANTUM II HYPERDRIVE
A hyperdrive immensely faster that the Quantum I hyperdrive, it achieves the second quantum rate of hyperspace travel, 1.25 minutes per light year. The Quantum II unit is enormous, barely fitting within a GP No. 4 hull.

RAMROBOT
Unmanned ramscoop exploration craft.

RAMSCOOP
Conical electromagnetic field of fusion ramship which accumulates interstellar hydrogen fuel; the toroids which generate such a field.

RAMSHIP
Starships that use magnetic fields to gather interstellar hydrogen, directing the gas into a fusion chamber which powers the ship. Although unable to exceed the speed of light, ramships often travel close to light-speed, and experience pronounced relativistic effects.

REACTION DRIVE
Any propulsion system which produces thrust by emitting a photon beam or expelling mass at sub-light velocities.

REACTIONLESS DRIVE
Any sub-light propulsion system which does not eject a stream of matter (or photons) to produce thrust, such as a gravity polarizer or a thruster.

RELATIVISTIC
Of or pertaining to velocities close to the speed of light; phenomenon which occur at such velocities, such as time-dilation.

REPAIR CENTER
A major maintenance and control center for Ringworld systems. At least one is known to exist beneath the Map of Mars.

RIM TRANSPORT SYSTEM
Partially-completed electromagnetic shuttle system along the top edge of the rim walls.

RIM WALLS
Parallel 1000 mile high walls rising all the way around both interior edges of Ringworld, preventing the escape of the atmosphere.

RINGWORLD ERA
That time in Known Space history when the existence of Ringworld became generally known. Usually dated from 2850, the year of the first Ringworld expedition. The existence of Ringworld is regarded as top secret by the governments of Earth and Kzin.

RINGWORLD LONGEVITY DRUG
The Ringworld longevity drug is much more powerful than boosterspice. One dose of the drug will incapacitate the subject for up to 60 days, but will retard aging for about 400 years, when another dose must be taken. The drug was originally synthesized from tree-of-life root, but later was lab synthesized. The remnants of the City Builder empire have lost the secret of its manufacture; they depend on their dwindling existing supply, and are

loath to sell even a single dose to anyone. Its effects on humans are not known.

RISHATHRA [ri-SHAH-thruh]
The City Builder term for sex with a partner not of one's own species but within the hominids.

SCRITH
Extremely dense, impenetrable, ultra-solid material used in the major construction of Ringworld.

SCRITH REPULSOR
Any MAGLEV material, motor, or vehicle held aloft by electromagnetic force directed against structural scrith.

SHAEFFER, BEOWULF
Crashlander pilot hired by the Puppeteers to test fly the first Quantum II hyperdrive ship to the edge of the galactic core in the 27th century; discovered the core radiation front.

SEA STATUE
Popular name for the first alien discovered on Earth, a Slaver (Thrint) in stasis.

SHADOW SQUARES
A linked loop of enormous, thin rectangular panels circling between Ringworld and its sun. They cast shadows on the surface of Ringworld to simulate night.

SINCLAIR MOLECULE CHAIN
An extremely tough, thin monofilament developed for use in ramship tow cables.

SINGULARITY
A discontinuity in hyperspace caused by a gravity well in normal space.

SLAVERS
An ancient race of powerfully telepathic aliens, the Thrint. Their ability to control other sentient beings allowed them to create a vast interstellar empire. They were wiped out n a galaxy-wide war with rebellious slave races.

SLAVER STASIS BOXES
Valued artifacts from the great ancient war between the Thrint and their slave races, in containers protected by stasis fields for safekeeping. Some of these boxes have been found by Known Space races. Their contents have included valuable and exotic technical items which have revolutionized the civilizations of Known Space.

SLAVER DISINTEGRATOR
Commonly used as a mining tool, this device also makes a powerful weapon. It suppresses the charge on the electron in normal matter.

SLAVER SUNFLOWER
A Tnuctipun engineered plant. Their highly reflective petals focus sunlight and the blossoms turn to track the sun. The plants can direct enough concentrated solar energy at moving targets to fry them. Large patches of sunflowers area a major menace in some regions of Ringworld, and are difficult to eradicate.

SLEEPING PLATES
Widely-used substitutes for beds, sleeping plates produce a gentle, contoured, zero-gee field usually designed to comfortably accommodate two occupants.

SLOWBOAT
Early human interstellar craft which carried its own fuel. Used before the development of safe ramships.

SOLAR FLARE
A tremendous outburst of charged particles which erupts with the power of billions of nuclear bombs. Most stars flare unpredictably–but Ringworld's sun can be made to flare upon command, to power the meteor defense system.

SOL
Earth's sun, a non-variable yellow-white star, spectral type G.

SPACECRAFT LANDING SYSTEM
A system of linear accelerator rings on the outer rim of Ringworld (six systems evenly spaced around the Ring), used to match an incoming vessel's velocity with Ringworld's rotation.

SPACEPORT LEDGE
Any of six 100 mile-wide landing shelves located at the end of each Spacecraft Landing System.

SPEAKER-TO-ANIMALS
See Chmee

SPECTRAL TYPE
Standard classification system for stars, based on temperature, size, composition, and other factors.

SPILL MOUNTAINS
30-40 mile high mountains standing against the base of the rim walls spaced at roughly 30,000 miles all the way around the Ring. They recirculate flup which spills over the tops of the mountains and releases moisture into the atmosphere.

SPINWARD
In the direction of rotation of Ringworld.

STAGE TREE
Tnuctipun-engineered plant which grows a sold-fuel rocket core, a relic of the Slaver empire; found on some Known Space worlds.

STARBOARD
To the right as one faces spinward on the surface of Ringworld.

STARSEEDS
Huge, mindless life-forms which migrate from the galactic core to the tips of the spiral arms, often followed by Outsider ships.

STARSEED LURES
A device which causes a star to emit signals which attract starseeds, said to have been invented by the Puppeteers.

STASIS FIELDS
Whether Slaver, Puppeteer, Kzinti, or human–stasis fields are time-retarding fields with a number of possible ratios of external to internal time rates. Beings or objects within a stasis field experience the passage of time at a significantly slower rate than the rest of the universe. Items have emerged from Slaver stasis boxes after billions of years which appear to have been stored only seconds before. Stasis fields have a perfectly reflective, shiny surface nearly invulnerable to outside damage. A stasis field will reflect deep-radar, which is how Slaver stasis boxes are discovered.

STEPPING DISCS
An advanced teleportation system designed and used

by the Puppeteers. It consists of flat, open disks. When one steps onto a transmitter disc, one immediately is transported to the next receiver disk.

SUPERCONDUCTOR
A substance offering nearly zero resistance to the flow of electric current; electronic devices incorporating superconductors can be extremely compact and efficient.

TANJ
Slang acronym formed from "There Ain't No Justice." An expletive.

TASP
A device to render threatening opponents completely helpless. The tasp fires an inductance-beam which stimulates the pleasure center of the brain creating an instant feeling of total and pure joy, ecstasy. Enough exposure to the tasp causes addiction making the victim an unwitting slave. Puppeteers usually carry a tasp surgically implanted along one of their necks.

THALLIUM OXIDE
A black, toxic, water-soluble powder which, as a soil additive, is necessary to the growth of a symbiotic virus in tree-of-life plants.

TIME DILATION
A relativistic effect which becomes important at velocities just below the speed of light. Shipboard time slows appreciably with respect to the rest of the universe.

THRINT
The Slavers' name for their own species.

THRUSTER
A reactionless drive that has replaced the fusion drive in most of Known Space. Fusion engines are still used on warships. Though a spacecraft may have a hyperdrive, it must have another drive with which to enter and exit gravity wells of stars and planets.

TNUCTIPUN [t'NUK-ti-pun]
A mysterious, ancient alien race of biological engineers and advanced technologists who led the rebellion against the Slavers.

TOTAL CONVERSION
Technique utilizing 100% matter-to-energy transformation for generating power. Though not now possessed by any species of Known Space, the secret once may have been discovered by the Tnuctipun.

TOROID
Large, doughnut-shaped electromagnetic loop used to generate ramscoop fields; also, general term for any vaguely doughnut-shaped structure.

TRANSFER BOOTHS
A teleportation system used by humans and some other species of Known Space. Transfer booths are about the size and shape of enclosed 20th century phone booths. To use a transfer booth, one enters the booth, closes the door, and punches up the coordinates of the desired destination. Teleportation is nearly instantaneous.

TREE-OF-LIFE
The plant whose root triggers the transformation of hominid breeders into protectors. It emits a strong smell which younger hominids find unpleasant, but which any hominid over the age of 40 finds irresistible.

TRIDEE
General term for mass market holographic imaging devices.

TRINOC [TRY-nok]
A methane breathing alien species of Known Space, first encountered by humans about 20 years before the events of the first Ringworld expedition.

TURN
The time it takes any one location on Ringworld to revolve once around its sun. One turn equals 7.5 Ringworld days, or 8.75 Earth days.

UNS
United Nations Standard. All UNS time measurements are Earth-relative.

VAMPIRE PERFUME
Vampire perfume is a powerful aphrodisiac, synthesized by City Builder from the scent glands of vampires. Exposure to vampire perfume causes nearly all hominids (humans included) to be hopelessly enthralled with the charms of the wearer.

VARIABLE SWORD
A hand weapon with variable length blade of fine wire, protected and made rigid by a stasis field. A glowing red ball marks the extended tip of the wire/blade.

WE MADE IT
A human colony world in the Procyon star system, 11.3 light years from Earth.

WIREHEAD
Current addiction addicts are known as wireheads. Such a person has had a wire surgically implanted on the back of his or her head. This wire connects directly with the pleasure center of the brain. Using a transformer known as a droud, a wirehead plugs himself into a current source and directly stimulates the brain's pleasure center, bringing uncontrolled bliss. Some wire addicts are dangerous and known as "live wires."

WU, LOUIS
First human to establish informal contact with the Trinoc. Chosen for the first expedition to Ringworld for his natural explorer skills; kidnapped for the second expedition.

WUNDERLAND
A human world in the Alpha Centauri system, the nearest colony to Earth, 4.3 light years distant. Wunderland is the longest-established human colony world with a light-gravity and benign climate and a history of political turmoil.

WUNDERLAND TREATYMAKER
An awesome weapon; an enormous duel-beam charge suppression device, a gigantic version of the Slaver disintegrator built on Wunderland and transported to Canyon. It was fired only once (at the end of the third Man-Kzin War). The two beams touched down thirty miles apart on the surface, bracketing the main Kzinti military installation and spaceport. A solid bar of lightning chewed twelve miles deep into the planet destroying an area the size of Baja California.

XENOLOGY
A general term for the study of aliens, alien cultures, and alien technologies.